PAINT THE TOWN DEAD

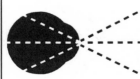This Large Print Book carries the Seal of Approval of N.A.V.H.

A JUDGE JACKSON CRAIN MYSTERY

PAINT THE TOWN DEAD

NANCY BELL

THORNDIKE PRESS

A part of Gale, Cengage Learning

GALE
CENGAGE Learning

Detroit • New York • San Francisco • New Haven, Conn • Waterville, Maine • London

LIBRARY OF CONGRESS CATALOGING-IN-PUBLICATION DATA

Bell, Nancy, 1932–
    Paint the town dead : a Judge Jackson Crain mystery / by Nancy Bell.
      p. cm. — (Thorndike Press large print mystery)
    ISBN-13: 978-1-4104-1123-5 (hardcover : alk. paper)
    ISBN-10: 1-4104-1123-0 (hardcover : alk. paper)
    1. Real estate agents—Crimes against—Fiction. 2. Women evangelists—Fiction. 3. Judges—Texas—Fiction. 4. City and town life—Texas—Fiction. 5. Large type books. I. Title.
    PS3552.E5219P35 2008b
    813'.54—dc22
                                    2008035380

Published in 2008 by arrangement with St. Martin's Press, LLC.

PAINT THE TOWN DEAD

CHAPTER ONE

Poplar Street was peaceful. Lined on both sides with elegant old houses, it was Post Oak's bastion of old-money opulence. At least that was the impression it gave. In fact, there was no old money in Post Oak. The town had only been established as a railway stop in the late nineteenth century, and most of the residents of Poplar Street were retirees in from Dallas looking for the simplicity of small-town living. Even though it had been established by horse thieves and carpetbaggers, the neighborhood still gave the newcomers a feeling of stability and old-world charm.

At dusk one windy day in March Benjy Rainey rode his bicycle home from school. He had been kept in once again for talking in class and was carrying a note from his teacher in his pocket. He rode as slowly as he could without falling over, because he dreaded getting home.

Angela Schultz slowed her Suburban in front of the Paschal house to drop off Missy Paschal. It was Angela's day to drive the team home after soccer practice. Missy was the last, and Angela was glad. She had a splitting headache, and the shrill voices of the preteen girls had not made it any better.

Across the street, a well-worn panel truck pulled into the driveway of one of the homes. Printed on its sides were these words:

DICKIE'S DELI
CUSTOM CATERING FOR ALL
OCCASIONS

This home was perhaps the most impressive on the street. Greek revival in style, it was surrounded on three sides by a wide veranda fronted by Doric columns. Red geraniums in black urns stood guard between the columns. The immense front door, painted turkey red, was topped by a leaded-glass fan light. A gravel path around one side of the house led to a smaller building out back. More gravel provided parking space for several cars. A sign on the door identified the place as the home of Del-Max Realtors. It was here that Dickie Deaver was going.

He got out and looked at the gray sky. A slow drizzle had started to fall and the wind had died down a little. Dickie decided that this was not enough moisture for any rain gear, only enough to run down your collar and fog up your glasses and make you downright miserable. He took a deep breath of the heavy air and opened the rear doors of the truck. He drew out an old gurney that he had purchased at the hospital's tag sale when he first started out in business and money was tight. It worked just fine and would carry more food than anything else he could purchase now that he could afford to. He had scrubbed the top thoroughly with Lysol and re-covered it with plastic, but he still wondered from time to time what that gurney had carried before he came to possess it. He started loading things on it: a large ice chest, several silver trays and bowls, and two one-gallon containers of iced tea. Pushing the gurney, which rattled and complained over the graveled ground, he headed toward the door of the office. Dickie had been asked to cater the monthly meeting of the Tri-County Realtors Association that was meeting that evening. He parked the gurney and rapped on the door.

He stood listening for a minute, and when

there was no answer, he rapped again. Still no answer. He put his ear against the door and listened for sounds of life inside, but all he heard was the ticking of a clock and the hum of the air-conditioning. He knocked again, this time pounding the door with the side of his fist. Shaking his head, he went back to the truck and picked up his cell phone from the front seat. He slid into the passenger's seat to get out of the rain, which was now coming down harder, and dialed a number. He waited for several rings. When the answering mechanism kicked in, he reported that he was waiting outside in the rain and asked why wasn't anybody there to meet him. Dickie shook his head and looked at his watch, obviously irritated that he had been stood up. Tom Delgado, the owner of the business, had told him specifically that the food was to be delivered at six o'clock sharp. It was now two minutes till. Dickie looked around and wondered what to do.

Just then a black BMW pulled up onto the gravel and a striking woman got out. She was wearing a black pantsuit that hugged her curves to perfection. Her hair was blond and pulled back from her face in a severe chignon. Her face would have been beautiful had she not had a perpetual pair of lines between her eyebrows and her perfect mouth not been turned down in a perpetual frown. She reached back into the car and got out a plastic rain hat, which she placed on her head. Then she trotted across the gravel as fast as she could in the spike heels she was wearing. It was Brenda Barns, one of Tom's agents.

"What's the matter, Dickie?" she said, noticing his puzzled expression.

"I've got the food here, and I can't get in," he replied. "Where do you reckon Tom's got off to?"

"He's not here?"

Dickie didn't think that needed an answer. He had no use for excessive conversation.

Brenda pulled a cell phone our of her purse and began to punch in numbers.

"No use. I already tried."

She flipped the tiny phone shut. "Never mind," she said. "I've got a key."

Brenda used her key to open the front door. The large room had obviously been set up for the meeting. The five agents' desks had been pushed against one wall and folding chairs were arranged in a circle around the space this provided. Two long folding tables were set against the back window wall waiting for the catered food. Dickie went to these tables and began unloading food while Brenda pushed open the door to Tom's office in the rear. Dickie was arranging sandwiches on a tray when he heard a scream.

"Oh, my God!"

He rushed back to see what was the matter. Brenda was standing at the open door to the office, her hand over her mouth. Dickie stood beside her. At first all he could see was Tom Delgado's sumptuous office: An antique oriental rug intricately patterned in red, gold, and blue covered the floor; a French sideboard on one side of the room held crystal decanters and glasses. On the opposite wall a glass-fronted bookcase held leather-bound books that were obviously put there for decorative purposes. Directly facing the door stood a huge and elegantly carved mahogany desk, and behind it was a high-backed leather chair. Slumped in the chair sat Tom Delgado. His face was in the palm of his right hand as if he were sitting and thinking. His left hand rested on top of a stack of papers on the desk and clutched a ballpoint pen. He might have been simply resting, maybe thinking about some problem connected with the pile of files on his desk. He might have been except for the small hole in his temple that oozed red-black blood.

Brenda slammed the office door. "Don't

go in," she said. "We've got to call the sheriff."

Later that evening Judge Jackson Crain was driving home through the dense fog that had rolled in to join the steady drizzle. He drove slowly down the darkened state highway leading to Post Oak. He and everybody else in town knew that Dinky Mackey never mended his fences, and that his cattle would, likely as not, be grazing along the road's right-of-way. As he made his way through the fog, Jackson thought of Lutie Fay Ivory standing in his bright kitchen fixing him one of her good meals; he also thought of the large Scotch and the Don Diego cigar he would enjoy after the meal. He was thinking fondly of that when he saw a black Ford Expedition with tinted windows bearing down on his rear bumper. The Expedition roared past just as a pickup truck pulled out of a side road. Jackson swerved onto the shoulder, spinning his tires and spewing gravel across his hood and windshield. He cursed. As the Expedition disappeared into the dusk, he saw the personalized license plate: GOD-WMAN. Mary Dobbs McDermott, the famous evangelist from Dallas. Jackson recognized the plate because she had been coming to Post

Oak a lot lately. Talk around town was that she was intent on saving the soul of Realtor Tom Delgado. Most people agreed that she had her work cut out for her, Tom being the cutthroat businessman that he was — and a womanizer to boot.

Jackson was the county judge of Post Oak County, Texas. He was returning from the annual regional meeting of county officials, where he had spent the entire day listening to boring speakers tell more than he wanted to know about county budgets, personnel problems, and road projects. This year's meeting had been held at Cypress Lake Lodge. Lunch had been cold fried catfish, bullet-hard hush puppies, and limp french fries. He sure hoped Lutie Fay had a good supper planned for him after he finished his Scotch. He pulled the car back onto the road and continued on his way, wondering why the lady preacher was in such a hurry.

Jackson, a widower, lived with his daughter, Patty, in the Queen Anne Victorian house he had grown up in. He pulled his car into the carport in back and, taking the steps two at a time, burst through the back door, tossing his briefcase on the bench in the hall.

Lutie Fay was peeling carrots at the sink when he got to the kitchen door. The room

14

smelled deliciously of roasting meat.

Jackson stood for a moment, taking in the sights and smells of the old kitchen that held so many memories for him. He had sat in his high chair at that table with the oilcloth cover while his mother and grandmother made preserves or put up fresh tomatoes and corn on summer days. Later, he had done his homework and eaten a thousand meals there. Lutie interrupted his reverie.

"Supper not ready yet. The roast got another thirty minutes to go."

"Good," Jackson said. "That'll give me time for a cigar before dinner. Where's Patty?"

"Up in her room. She say she's got a government test tomorrow."

When Jackson got to the front hall he wondered how Patty could be studying. The whole house reverberated with the booming bass of a rock band. "Turn it down!" he yelled up the stairs. The sound grew softer, but not by much. Jackson retrieved his paper from the hall table and went into his den, where he poured himself a stiff Scotch and dropped into his old leather chair with a sigh.

The phone rang. Jackson picked it up reluctantly.

"Judge Crain, this here's Gibbs."

Leonard J. Gibbs was the sheriff of Post Oak County.

"What's up?" Jackson asked.

"Judge, would you come over to Tom Delgado's house? You'd be doing me a big favor."

"What for?"

"Delgado's been murdered."

Jackson let out a long sigh. "I'll be there," he said.

Before he left, Jackson went upstairs to talk to his daughter. He found Patty sprawled on her bed with the TV and the radio both blaring at the same time. She was listlessly thumbing through a schoolbook opened in front of her.

Jackson crossed the room and dropped a kiss on the mass of brown curls that covered her head. "Hey, kid. Learned anything yet?" He looked pointedly at the radio.

"That's sarcasm, isn't it?" Patty reached across to the radio and switched it off.

"Yeah, probably. It's hard for an old man to understand how anybody could think, much less learn, with all that noise."

Patty rolled over and got off the bed. She hugged Jackson around the waist and looked up at him. "You could help me, you know. I'm studying for a government test, and since your job is in government . . ."

"I must know all about it?"

"Yeah, Daddy." She looked up at him with what she no doubt imagined was a captivating smile.

"You women are all alike. You think you can twist any man around your finger — even your old dad." He disentangled her arms from his waist and turned toward the door. "I'll make you a deal. I've got to go back out. If you'll concentrate and study until you think you've got it down, I'll go over the material with you in the morning before school."

"Deal," she said, clicking the radio back on.

Jackson went down to the kitchen. Lutie Fay had taken the roast out of the oven and placed it on the table, where it rested, mahogany brown, oozing delectable juices and filling the room with its tantalizing scent. She was stirring gravy on the stove.

"I have to go out," Jackson announced.

Lutie Fay turned. "You ain't."

"Afraid so. There's been a murder."

Lutie Fay nodded. "Reckon you better go then. I'll fix you a plate."

"Leave it on top of the microwave." Jackson turned reluctantly away from the kitchen and went out to his car.

■ ■ ■ ■

Driving through the damp streets, past homes where at this hour people would be having their dinners, watching the news, doing homework, Jackson thought uneasily about how fragile life was, how susceptible we all were to sudden outbursts of violence that often led to tragedy. Hale and hearty Tom Delgado was the last person you'd expect to be struck down. Here was a guy who had it all: a thriving business, a doting wife, respect in the community. If he wasn't safe from such an outrage, was anybody?

Jackson remembered Tom coming into his office, what was it? Ten years ago? It was when he first came to town, and he was going around introducing himself to, Jackson supposed, all the people in town who might be able to swing business his way. He was a neat little man. That had been Jackson's first impression. The second was that he was slick. His hair was as black and shiny as patent leather, his complexion was swarthy, and his eyes black and sharp. He smiled showing white teeth and extended his hand.

"Tom Delgado," he said. "I'm new in town, and I'm told that if I want to get anywhere in business around here, I'd better make friends with Judge Jackson Crain."

Jackson smiled to himself. He had had a feeling that Delgado used this opening remark with everyone he met.

"Have a seat," Jackson had said, indicating the red leather clients chair in front of his desk. "Exactly where do you want to go into business?"

"Real estate," Tom said. "The wife and I have bought the old Himes house on Poplar Street. Know it?"

Jackson knew it well. The Himeses had been a founding family of Post Oak. Old man Himes had made his money in railroading. The house had been divided into apartments after the last of the Himes family died. It had sat empty for the last five years.

"Restoring it?" he asked.

"Oh, yeah," Tom had said. "My wife's from a rich family. The Wynns from Dallas. She won't have anything but the best. And I wouldn't want her to have anything but the best."

"Tell me about your plans," Jackson said.

"All kinds of real estate, commercial and family homes. Recreational for sure. I understand the lakes around here draw people from all over for primary homes as well as second homes."

"That's a fact," Jackson said.

"And farms and ranches, of course. Right now, I'm building a staff of professional agents. I'm looking for folks who specialize in different areas. And, Judge, that's what I'm here for. I'm wondering if you know any agents who might be interested in locating with a broker who'll back them all the way, and who believes the sky's the limit."

Jackson had assured him that he didn't know a soul.

Delgado had stood up and extended his hand. "Well, Judge, if you think of anybody, here's my card. The wife and I are staying at the Holiday Inn in Longview until our house is finished."

That had been the first and last conversation Jackson had had with Tom Delgado, but he heard around town that he had indeed put together a staff and was outpacing every other broker in a three-county area.

And now he had been murdered.

The sheriff's car and the EMS ambulance were already there when Jackson pulled into the Delgados' driveway. Jackson got out and walked toward the office, where outside lights had been turned on. The sheriff came to meet him as he pushed open the door.

"How did it happen?" Jackson asked.

"Shot through the head," Sheriff Gibbs

20

replied. "Small-caliber pistol, I'm guessing. We ain't found a weapon."

"Any forensics?"

"Nope. No powder marks around the wound, no fingerprints that we know of. The state boys have already dusted the place and left.

Just then Dooley Burns, the sheriff's deputy, ambled over. Dooley was not too bright, but the sheriff kept him on because he was dependable and loyal. Dooley was holding up a pencil with a metal cylinder hanging from it. "Found this here, Sheriff. Hey, Judge."

Jackson nodded at Dooley and peered at the object. "Could be a . . ."

"Silencer," the sheriff said. He pulled a plastic Baggie out of a canvas bag on the desk. "Slide it in here, Doo. Where'd you find it."

"Over yonder by the window." Dooley gestured with his arm. "What'd you say that thing was?"

"A silencer for a gun," Jackson explained.

"So it won't make no noise?"

The sheriff's face turned an alarming color of red. "Yes, you knucklehead. So it won't make no noise! Why else would it be called a 'silencer'?" He turned to Jackson. "Reckon why them state boys missed that?"

Jackson shook his head. He turned to the EMS crew, who had loaded the covered body onto a stretcher. He spoke to Amy Tubbs, tall, black, and exceedingly efficient. "What do you know, Amy?"

Amy stood with her hand on the stretcher next to the body. "Apparently Dickie Deaver and Brenda Barns found him. Dickie had come to bring food for the Realtors' meeting tonight. He couldn't get in until Brenda arrived with a key. They looked in his office and there he was, sitting at his desk."

"Where are they now?"

"You'll have to ask the sheriff that. They were gone when we got here." She moved toward the door. "We need to get out of here, Judge. We've got another call to make."

"Right." Jackson stood aside. "Where are you taking him?"

"Oh, he'll go to the hospital morgue so Dr. Chu can go over the body. After that, I suppose the hospital will call the funeral home to come get him."

Jackson looked around the room. Nothing seemed to be out of order. He walked over to take a look at the papers on the desk. An open real estate contract was directly in front of the chair. Jackson leaned down to read it. The principals were people he didn't know, but the property being sold was the

Harrison farm east of town. Using a pencil eraser, he moved that aside and looked at several other documents stacked under it: more contracts, a survey, and a financial statement. Nothing the least bit out of the ordinary for a Realtor to have.

"Judge." The sheriff was coming toward him. "Miz Delgado's sittin' on the porch over yonder. Miz Applewhite's come over to be with her. Reckon you could have a talk with her?"

"Sure," Jackson said. "Have you questioned her?"

The sheriff colored. "Not too much. Truth is, I'm . . . well, I'm a little bit what you'd call *uncomfortable* around these folks. It's all that money, if you catch my drift."

"I'll talk to her."

"Thanks, Judge. Me and Dooley's going to finish up here and get on back to the jail. I reckon we could have a talk first thing in the morning?"

Jackson nodded. "I've got a ten o'clock appointment. I'll come on by the jail on my way to the office."

Jackson walked up the path to the screened-in porch at the back of the house, where he found Dovie Delgado and Mae Applewhite sitting in wicker chairs. Mae was talking, as usual, and Dovie was listening and nodding from time to time. She appeared unnaturally calm considering the circumstances.

"Hi, ladies. Can I come in?" Jackson stood just outside the screen door.

"Who is it?" he heard Dovie ask Mae.

"It's the judge. Judge Crain," Mae answered.

"Come in, Judge," Dovie called. "Come and have a glass of tea with us."

When he got inside Jackson noticed that the two were sipping iced tea. He also noticed an opened bottle of bourbon on the table between them. Dovie saw the look. "Perhaps you'd like a real drink." Her voice was deep, almost mannish.

Jackson declined the offer. "Lutie Fay's got a fine supper waiting for me at home. Mrs. Delgado, how are you doing? Is there anything I can do for you?" He studied the woman.

About forty-five, she was short and stocky of build, but toned and tanned from days spent golfing and gardening. Her hair was mousy brown and cut short. She wore tailored jeans with a white cotton shirt. Expensive-looking loafers clad her exceptionally small feet.

"No, I'm fine." She sipped her tea. "Just talking to Mae here about the funeral. When can we have it?"

"Soon, I imagine," Jackson answered. "They're taking him to the hospital for a going-over by the medical examiner. After that, the hospital will call the funeral home. Are you sure I can't help?" he asked again.

"Nope. The funeral will have to be top-drawer. Tom would have wanted it that way. And, of course, everybody in town will be there. We'll have the church decorated with all white flowers. Mae, would you do me a great favor?"

"Of course," Mae said.

"Would you contact both the florist shops and tell them that I want only white flowers? Tell them that when anybody calls in to order, to make sure that they only send white. I think white flowers are the prettiest kind, don't you?" She addressed that to Jackson, who was getting increasingly uneasy. He wondered whether her tea might be laced with bourbon.

"Definitely the prettiest. Now, Miss Dossie, if it's not too painful, I need to ask you a few questions."

"Not at all. Ask away."

"What were you doing this afternoon?"

"Well, let's see. I played golf at the club until four. Had a terrible game. I can't seem to get rid of this slice I've developed. I'm

25

going to have to take a few lessons, I guess. After that the girls and I had a glass of wine in the bar. Now, let me see. Oh, yes. I stopped in at Lucy's Boutique for a pair of nylons, and then came home."

"What time was that?"

"Around five thirty, I guess. I had a shower and a nap. When I came downstairs, I heard Brenda Barns pounding on my door. She told me poor old Tommy had been shot. Well, all hell broke loose then. The sheriff came with his siren making all that noise — and then the ambulance. I just came up here to watch the commotion. They didn't need me getting in the way."

"Was anybody in the house with you?"

"No, I was alone. Fayrene, our wonderful cook, had gone home early because Tommy was having his meeting, and I was just going to fix myself a light supper and go to bed early."

Jackson got to his feet. "Well, that about does it, then. You call me if I can help you in any way. Okay?"

Dovie stood, too. "It's been a pleasure talking to you." She said it as lightly as if she had been talking to a casual caller.

Mae Applewhite followed Jackson down the stairs. "Judge, does she seem right to you?"

"No," Jackson said. "She may be in shock. Has the doctor seen her?"

"She wouldn't have it. Says she's fine."

"Are you going to stay with her?"

"If she'll let me. She mentioned that her housekeeper will be here bright and early tomorrow morning. Frankly, I don't think she wants me to stay."

CHAPTER TWO

When Jackson got back home he went up to his room and sat down on the side of the bed. He picked up the phone and dialed Mandy d'Alejandro's cell phone. He waited for several minutes, and when she didn't answer, waited a minute more for the answering device to come on. Nothing. Shaking his head, he hung up.

Mandy was the woman Jackson hoped to marry, and the sooner the better. The problem was, he hadn't been able to get her to set a date. She had gone to Victoria in South Texas to care for her grandmother, who was recovering from a stroke. Jackson missed her like crazy. He hung up the phone and peeled off his shirt. He stepped out of his pants, hung them over the back of a chair, and climbed into bed.

He lay there thinking about Mandy. He had called three nights in a row with the same results. Maybe her grandmother had taken a turn for the worse and had had to go to the hospital. Still, he was damn sure Mandy could find the time to call and let him know. He made up his mind to start calling all the hospitals in Victoria tomorrow. Something must be very wrong.

His mind went back to the first day he met her. It was the day of the ribbon cutting for the new office of the Main Street project. He didn't know it at the time, but Mandy had moved to town to run that operation. Patty was in the junior high band, and Jackson had promised to stop by to hear her play. The day had been beautiful when he walked across the street from the courthouse to the little yellow house that had been converted into the Main Street offices.

He remembered that he had grinned as the band hobbled through a medley of Sousa marches. He had winked at Patty, whose face was contorted into a fierce frown as she concentrated on the music sheet attached to her French horn. When the last cymbal crashed, Mayor McGonigal ascended the steps to stand on the front porch that would serve as a stage for the ceremony. He issued his standard ribbon-cutting speech. The mayor was eighty-four and had been reelected more times than anyone could remember. He always gave the same speech, and when he remembered, he inserted the correct name of the business being honored.

As the speech droned on, Jackson watched the young woman awaiting her turn to speak. She wore a red-and-white scarf around her neck, which complemented her Latin features. The large hoops on her ears would have been gaudy on most women. They seemed to have been made for her.

After the ribbon was cut, Jackson pushed his way to the front of the crowd and stood beside Horace Kincaid, who was busily snapping pictures for next week's local paper. He gave Jackson a shove.

"Stand over there by the mayor and Miz d'Alejandro." He gestured with his camera. "I want all the dignitaries in this shot."

After the photo was shot, Jackson turned to her. "Welcome to Post Oak." He wondered where he had ever seen eyes so clear.

"Thank you."

As the crowd moved away, Jackson lingered to talk to her.

He smiled as he remembered how awkward he had felt. "Uh," he had said, "can I buy you something to drink?"

She smiled. "I'd love it."

He had taken her to Minton's Rexall, where they had a soda fountain. He remembered that he had complimented her on her accent. "Charming," he had said.

She had told him that her father's family had been in the States for many generations, but that her mother had come from Chihuahua at an early age. Her parents had spoken only Spanish.

"You must miss your family."

"Yes, I do," she had responded. "Hispanic families are very close — closer, I think, than Anglos."

"I'll take your word for it. We don't get many Mexican Americans in East Texas."

She had smiled wryly. "I've noticed. Little children stare at me."

"You're kidding!"

"Yes, I'm kidding." She had grinned wickedly at him.

Jackson held open the heavy glass door and followed her into Minton's drugstore.

"What would you like?" He guided her into a rear booth.

"An ice cream sundae," she said immediately.

"Then I'll join you."

He had gone to the counter to place their orders. He remembered watching as Brittany Bean, the teenager behind the counter, had scooped large dips of vanilla ice cream into lily-shaped sundae glasses and poured on thick dark chocolate syrup. She had added whipped cream, and finished with a red cherry. She put them on a tray with spoons, glasses of ice water, and napkins.

Back at the table they had both dug into their sundaes, feeling like kids again.

Jackson sighed in his bed. Lord, he missed her.

"Daddy, you woke me up when you came in. I was like, where has he been?" Patty was sitting at the breakfast table eating cereal when Jackson entered the kitchen the next morning.

"Sorry, Sis. Couldn't be helped. Did you get through studying?"

Patty drained the orange juice from her glass. "Yep. Where were you, anyway?"

Lutie Faye set a cup of coffee in front of Jackson. "You want pancakes or eggs?"

"Pancakes, if you've got them." Lutie Faye's pancakes were lighter than air, and delicious. He turned to Patty. "Honey, do you know Mr. Tom Delgado?"

"Seen his signs," Patty said. "Isn't he the real estate man?"

"That's right. Well, he was murdered last night."

Lutie turned away from the griddle. "Say what?"

"Somebody shot him in the head in his office," Jackson said. He had decided long ago not to try to shield Patty from the truth. In this small town she would find out soon enough. Better it come from him.

"My cousin Fayrene works for Miz Delgado," Lutie said. "I better call her and see what can I do."

"Good idea," Jackson said, admiring the plate of hotcakes she set before him. He ate quickly and drained his coffee. "I've got to get going." He looked at Patty. "Want me to go over your school stuff with you before I go?"

She pointed to her head. "Got it all up here," she said. "I'm acing this thing."

"Go, girl," Jackson said. He kissed the top of her head. "No need to make lunch for me, Lutie. I'll just grab something in town."

Lutie nodded. "Supper'll be at six. I got choir practice tonight."

The Knitters' Nook stands on Main Street just between the antique shop and the post office. The building had begun life as a general store back when the town was founded. It had been the heart of Post Oak life at one time, supplying farmers and

33

townspeople with all the necessities of life. Then, sometime in the forties, after A & P came to town, the old general store closed its doors. The building was subdivided into two long and narrow spaces. One side became the post office, the other a small café. By the time the Archer sisters, Jane and Esther, purchased the property, it had stood empty for more than ten years. Many more years of grease and grime had accumulated on the floors and walls and on the bay window that looked out onto the sidewalk. A narrow shelf meant to display merchandise was tucked into the curve of that window.

The sisters cleaned for weeks. Elvis Hicks was hired with his pickup to cart off ten loads of trash from the concrete floors before Jane and Esther could even think of getting out their brooms and mops. As soon as Elvis left with the last load, they set to work. When they finished, the concrete floors had been freshly painted with a cheery blue and covered with sisal mats. The one window, now draped in white lace, sparkled. And the little shelf in front displayed all manner of items made and consigned by the creative women of Post Oak: dolls dressed in hand-sewn clothes; afghans; doilies; quilts; embroidered place mats and napkins. Jane and Esther also sold the raw materials for their customers; yarns, needlepoint supplies, pattern books, and needles of all kinds. This was where they made their money. Since most of their customers were creators themselves, they weren't the least bit interested in buying what someone else had made. So the finished products languished in the window waiting for some souvenir-seeking tourist to happen by. Inside, bins and shelves spilled over with even more merchandise. The place was now neat and cozy and the perfect gathering place for the ladies of Post Oak. Here the latest news was delivered, dissected, sorted, and flung back onto the street for popular consumption.

On a certain day, precisely at nine, Esther and Jane arrived at the shop and turned the cardboard sign in the window to OPEN. Esther hurried to put on some coffee while Jane turned on the lights. The bell tinkled on the door and Mae Applewhite bustled in.

"You're never going to believe what's happened," she said without even a hello first.

Jane and Esther came and stood behind the counter.

"All ears," snapped Jane, who had served time in the navy in her youth.

"Tom Delgado — you know who he is, that real estate man that lives across the street from me — well, he got shot dead last night . . . in his office." Mae stopped for breath.

Esther, small and feminine, turned pale and put her hand to her breast. "Lord have mercy," she breathed. "How?"

Mae lowered her voice and moved in closer. "It was murder," she whispered.

"Come 'round back and sit down," Jane said. "I'll pour us all some coffee and you tell us all about it."

Mae raised the hinged section of the counter and squeezed through.

"How is Dossie taking it?" Esther wanted to know, when they were seated around the little wooden table in back. "She must be just about killed!"

"Not so much," Mae said. "I stayed all night over at her house. She acted like it had never even happened, just kept talking about him like he was still among the living."

"Who did it?" Jane wanted to know.

Just then the bell tinkled again, and Annabeth Jones came in for a skein of navy blue knitting worsted. Mae repeated the story to her.

Annabeth had a theory. "I'll bet it was a

jealous husband," she said. She dropped her voice to a whisper. "You all knew he was running around on her?"

"Peggy Panther's grandson saw him with that blond Barns woman that works for him out at that tavern out on the lake, the Flying Fish. She said he said they were hugged up together like a couple of lovebirds."

"That's just nasty," Esther said.

"Well, I've got my suspicions about him and that lady preacher he's so taken with," Jane said. "I mean he *was* so taken with."

"Well, all I can say is, I'm sorry for Dossie," Mae said. "She's the kind of woman that can't be alone. Needs a man, don't you know."

"Wait a minute," Jane said, ignoring that. "Maybe it was a jealous husband — or boyfriend. Hold on, something's coming to me." She squeezed her eyes tight and thought. "Of course!" she said, opening her eyes. "That strange man, you know the one I mean, Deke something-or-other. Looks like a zombie, the way he walks."

"I know who you're talking about. Deke Slade," Mae said. She giggled. "Jane, you're so bad. Zombie, indeed!"

"Well, he does," Jane said. "Haven't you noticed he never swings his arms when he walks?"

"Well, I think he's cute," Esther said. "He's got the most beautiful eyes."

"I've got to go," Mae said. "I'm going to check on Dossie. Now, you all be sure and let me know if you hear anything. You hear me?"

Sheriff Leonard J. Gibbs was a man of medium height, red faced and square shaped. He was nearing the end of his second term as sheriff of Post Oak County, and would be glad to get back to farming when that term came to an end. At one time he had thought that he would never want to farm again, but two terms in law enforcement had made the risky, weather-dependent life of a farmer look better every day. Besides, he would soon be able to draw his Social Security checks to help out in the lean years. His wife, Norma Jean, concurred wholeheartedly. She would gladly give up the little apartment attached to the jail for a small farmhouse with room to plant some flowers around the door.

Sheriff Gibbs was sitting at the kitchen table in his apartment behind the jail finishing his second cup of coffee. Norma Jean was at the sink loading the dishwasher. Jackson tapped on the door, and Norma Jean hurried to answer it, first peeking through the little window at the top to see who it was. When you lived in the jail, you could never be too careful.

"Come on in, Judge," she said, throwing the door wide open. "You want some coffee? Just made a fresh pot."

"Thanks, Norma Jean. You make the best coffee in town." He winked at the sheriff.

"Don't let it go to your head, honey," the sheriff said. "He says that to everybody. I even heard him say it to old Rip Clark over at the Wagon Wheel — and everybody knows his coffee tastes like pond scum."

Jackson looked at his watch. "Can't stay long," he said. "Did you interview Dickie — or the Barns woman?"

"Not much." The sheriff held out his mug to his wife for a refill. "They were both so shook up they could barely think straight."

Jackson shook his head. To his way of thinking, that would have been the best time to get the truth out of them — if they knew anything. If they had been involved in the murder, giving them time to devise a story was a big mistake.

"Want me to talk to them?"

"I'd be much obliged if you would. I've got a funeral to patrol and old Dooley's off sick."

Just then, the doorbell rang. Norma Jean

went to answer it, and in walked Dooley.

The sheriff just shook his head.

"Felt better, so I come on in. Could I please have some of that coffee, Miz Gibbs?"

"Help yourself, Dooley." Norma Jean had left the kitchen and was now sorting clothes in the adjoining laundry room.

Dooley poured his coffee and brought it to the table. He drained it in one gulp and then reached into his shirt pocket, pulled out a purple toothpick, and clamped it in his mouth.

The sheriff rolled his eyes. "Pretty fancy toothpick you got there. Where'd it come from?"

Dooley took the toothpick out of his mouth and stared dumbly at it. "Search me," he said, and went back to chewing.

Jackson got back to business. "Any prints on the silencer?" he asked.

"Lots, but they were all smudged," the sheriff said. "Not a good print in the bunch." He shifted his considerable bulk to a more comfortable position in his chair and lit a cigarette. "We dusted the whole place. Only good prints we got were Tom's. Tough luck."

Jackson nodded. "Well, I've got to get to work. "I'll let you know what I find out from Dickie and Brenda."

Jackson left the jail and walked across the concrete parking lot to the courthouse. He went up the stairs to the second floor, breathing in the familiar smell of the old building. He pushed open his office door and was greeted by a barrage of cursing. Nothing startling about that. It was only Edna Buchanan, his salty-tongued secretary. She was talking on the telephone.

"I've got to go, you bastard. The judge just came in. But you wait 'til I get home, and I'll kick your ass 'til your hat flies off!"

Edna listened for half a minute. "Now you listen to me, you old bald-headed son of a bitch, if I come home and that mess is not cleaned up, I'll snatch out what little hair you've got left." She slammed down the phone.

"What's old Grover done now?" Jackson asked.

Edna turned in her stenographer's chair. "The stupid son of a bitch has dug up my rose bed to put in a damn dirt-bike track. He's gone and got him this old secondhand bike, and he thinks he's Evel Knievel or something."

Jackson grinned at that. "Well, it could be worse. He could be out getting drunk and chasing women."

Edna snorted. "Him? Hell, Jackson, the

41

dumb-ass wouldn't know what to do with one if he caught one. And as for gettin' drunk, he done enough of that when he was young to last him a lifetime."

"Somebody shot Tom Delgado last night."

"Say what?"

"Somebody killed Tom Delgado."

"That slick-talking real estate guy?"

"He's the one."

"Well, tell me more. Where did it happen?"

"At his office. Dickie, the caterer, and Brenda Barns found him. Sheriff called me, and I went out there."

"Do they have any idea who did it?"

"Not yet. They didn't leave any prints or any other evidence — except a silencer for a gun." He paused. "And it didn't give us any good prints."

"You sound just like a lawman."

Jackson thought about that. "Guess I do."

"Jackson, how come, do you think, we have so many people getting murdered in this little old town?"

"Beats me. Crime's just rampant everywhere these days."

"Yeah, but we don't have any gangs here, or organized crime."

"You might be surprised at what goes on in this area. I happen to know there are meth labs hidden in the woods in this county."

"Just like they used to have whiskey stills." Jackson nodded.

"Well, here's my next question. Why the hell do you have to get involved in every one of them? Last time I looked, you were the county judge, not the sheriff. What's wrong with Gibbs that he can't handle his own business?"

Jackson sat down in one of the guest chairs and crossed his legs. "Am I neglecting things around here?"

"Hell, no. You're the best thing that's ever happened to this courthouse. I'm just wondering . . ."

"Okay, think back. The first murder I got involved in was when my wife's sister got killed. Remember, my brother-in-law was the prime suspect."

"Yeah. I do remember."

Jackson went on. "The second was a good friend of mine. And his daughter was Patty's best friend."

"Oh, yeah. The barber. So, okay, what the hell is Tom Delgado to you? Why this one?"

Jackson pulled a cigar out of his pocket, sniffed it, and then put it back. "It just interests me, that's all."

"Goddamn it, Jackson. There's more."

"You don't know when to quit, do you? Okay. When I was a young man, I wanted to go into police work — as a career, you know. Maybe the FBI or the Texas Rangers."

"Your daddy, the old judge, would've had a cow."

"Exactly. He wanted me to follow in his footsteps, go into law — not law enforcement."

"Well, your daddy was right. You could run for DA, you know."

"I guess." Jackson had thought of that and rejected the idea. He looked out the window, remembering a time long ago. His father, the old judge Crain, had been a lawyer of the old school, steeped in the majesty of the law and bound by the long-dead ethical standards of the profession. Jackson had never shared his father's dedication. Once he thought he wanted to go into police work. His father had looked at him as if he had announced that he wanted to run off and join the circus.

"You want to be a cop?"

"Yes, sir."

Jackson blushed, at the memory. He had wished he had kept his mouth shut. It had always been assumed that he would go to law school and follow in his father's foot-steps.

"Dad, this doesn't mean I won't go to law school. I could use that in law enforcement, couldn't I? I want to work on a big-city police force, maybe be chief some day." He remembered that long-ago day sitting on the edge of the sofa and looking earnestly at his father, hoping for some sign of under-standing. "It's just, well, crime . . . I don't know. It fascinates me. Always has."

"You think it's like the cop shows on television."

"No, sir. I don't, really. I'm not that stupid, Dad."

"Well, that's too bad, because I've heard that they won't take you for a cop if your IQ is much over average. Unfortunately, yours is 155. You can't qualify."

"I don't believe that, Dad."

"You can check it out."

"Then I'll join the FBI."

"Well, son, you're only sixteen. As long as you say you'll go to law school, we can decide on this later. I predict you'll forget all about this." The judge had picked up his paper and disappeared behind it.

Out on the courthouse lawn, he saw Raz Ochoa, the courthouse custodian, cleaning out the round flower bed around the flag pole, getting it ready for spring planting.

Jackson's mind went again to the past. His father had been wrong. He had never forgotten his passion for law enforcement. Until his third year at university, he had fully intended to move toward that goal. Then his father had his first heart attack. After that, the once powerful man seemed to shrink before Jackson's eyes until, by the time Jackson passed his bar exam, there was no choice but to come back home. Otherwise, the practice his father had worked so hard to build would have been lost.

He came back to the present. "Who's my ten?" he asked Edna.

She looked at the calendar on her desk. "Oh, yeah. It's old man Rice. He wants to sell off a piece of land he owns out on Broken Arrow Road."

Jackson went into his office and sat at his desk, still thinking about the direction his life had taken. Did he miss his first choice of a profession? Not really, he decided. His work was interesting, for the most part. His law practice was limited to property law, divorces, and probate matters, and that could get boring at times. He would like to have a criminal practice, but that was out because of his status as a judge. Maybe he should run for DA.

Just then, Edna stuck her head in the door. "Mr. Rice is here."

The rest of the day was busy. Jackson didn't have time to think about Tom Delgado's murder or his promise to the sheriff to interview Dickie and Brenda. When he pulled into his driveway at 5:30 he was, once again, thinking about a Scotch and a cigar before dinner. Once again, he was thwarted.

Lutie Faye was at the stove frying chicken. "Dinner be ready in a half hour," she said over her shoulder.

"No problem. I'll just . . ."

Then he noticed the three children sitting on stools around the island. They stared at him with round, black eyes — two little girls about six, with skin the color of coffee with cream and their hair in tight braids, and a boy, maybe two years older, with a scowl on his face.

Lutie turned and swept her hand, still holding the fork she had been using to turn the chicken, toward the kids. "This here's Corolla and Camry, the twins, and this is their brother, Tercel. Y'all say hi to Judge Crain."

"Hi," they said in unison.

"Hi back at you," Jackson said.

47

"I need for you to do me a big favor," Lutie said.

Jackson looked at her suspiciously. "What?"

"I need for you to take these kids home to their mama. It's my niece, Cookie. You know her. She works for old Miz Kruger."

"I know Cookie," Jackson said. "I got her divorce for her."

"Cookie's car's in the shop," Lutie said, anticipating Jackson's next question. "I been keepin' the kids after school since Miz Kruger got so bad, on account of Cookie likes to stay with her until the night nurse gets there at seven."

"Uh-huh. Where do they live?"

"Oh, it's not too far," Lutie said almost breezily. "Only about three miles out on Farm Road 3002."

In five minutes Jackson had the twins buckled into the backseat, with Tercel up front with him, and they were driving as fast as good sense would allow out Farm Road 3002. It was dusk. The shadows from the round hay bales were long; the fields were tinged with pink from the rays of the setting sun. He could hear Camry and Corolla whispering to each other in the backseat. Tercel sat silent and stern in the front.

"There it is," Tercel said, pointing. "The road where that big old tree is."

Jackson turned the car down the road the boy had indicated and pulled to a stop in front if a small white frame house. Cookie, about thirty, tall, willowy, and light-skinned, immediately opened the door.

"Thanks, Judge," she said. "You're a lifesaver."

"It's nothing." Jackson mumbled the lie. "How's Mrs. Kruger?"

"About gone, I think," she said. "I don't see how she can hold on much longer. She's ninety, you know, and has pneumonia in both lungs."

"Where's Roxanne? Hasn't she come home?" Jackson referred to the Krugers' only child, a daughter.

"She'll be here as soon as she can. She had a big, important show at a gallery in New York. There was no way she could get here right away. Her mama understands. Roxanne's a real famous artist up there. Mrs. Kruger told me her paintings sell for five figures. Isn't that over ten thousand?" Cookie shook her head in amazement. "I just hope and pray she makes it here on time."

The Krugers were not local to the area. They had moved to Post Oak in the seventies. The Kruger family had immigrated to Texas sometime in the nineteenth century, along with a great influx of German immigrants who had settled in the hill country of central Texas. The family was well known around the state for having made a fortune in cattle and oil. Old Wilhelm Kruger had served as governor in the twenties, during a time when corruption in state politics was the order of the day. His one term in office was remembered in the history books for its blatant use of graft and cronyism. The family had been living that down ever since. Now, having given away a fortune to various civic and academic causes, they were famous for their philanthropy.

Although Roxanne was near his age, Jackson had not known her well. Her parents had sent her back east to prep school and college. Jackson remembered her as a tall, mousy girl who appeared to be painfully shy. Roxanne had attended art school after college and, from all accounts, pursued a successful career as an artist.

"Well, hang in there," Jackson said to Cookie.

"Thanks, Judge," she answered. "I owe you — big time!"

She doesn't know the half of it, Jackson thought, as he turned the car around. He only hoped Lutie Faye had dinner on the table when he got home.

Luck was with him this time. When he walked into the kitchen Lutie was just pouring cream gravy into a bowl. She set it down beside a steaming mound of mashed potatoes. The chicken, crisp and golden, lay on a platter nearby. Biscuits, sliced tomatoes, and field peas made up the rest of the meal. Patty was already seated at the table. He looked questioningly at her.

"Aced it," she said with a grin. "I'm going to be a lawyer like you when I get out of school." She paused. "Or maybe I'll go on *American Idol* and be a recording star."

"The world's your oyster." Jackson smiled fondly at her. "And you've got plenty of time to decide."

Patty giggled. "The world's my oyster? Daddy, where do you come up with that stuff? I don't even like oysters."

Jackson smiled ruefully. "It's just an old expression my mother used to say," he said. "Means you can be anything you please."

But Patty had lost interest. She was enthusiastically biting down on a drumstick.

Later that night Jackson tried calling Mandy again. This time she picked up after four rings. Jackson could hear talking and music in the background.

"Jackson!" she said, speaking loudly over the noise.

"What's going on?" Jackson asked.

"What do you mean? Oh, you hear the noise, don't you? Well, Tía Elena is sitting with Mamacita, so I came out for a while — with the girls."

"Good. I know you needed a break. Well, go back and play. We'll talk tomorrow."

There was a fraction too long a pause before she said, "Yes, of course. Good-bye Jackson."

Jackson got into bed with a frown on his face. Something was not right, and he felt helpless to do anything about it, as she was four hundred miles away. A niggling suspicion entered his mind. Maybe she wasn't telling him the truth. Maybe her grandmother wasn't sick at all. Maybe she never intended to come home. No, he told himself. You're just imagining things. Mandy was as straightforward a woman as he had ever met. If anything was wrong in their relationship, she would tell him. He remembered the time he had gotten busy at the office and forgotten a date with her. He smiled to himself as he remembered it. She had given him a piece of her mind in spades, throwing in a few Spanish words for good measure. No, everything was fine, and she would be home as soon as she could. He vowed to ask her to marry him. It was high time they tied the knot.

CHAPTER THREE

The next morning dawned clear and warm. Jackson decided to walk to work. He went down his front steps and turned toward town. His neighbor Ham Boyd was out front picking up his paper. He waved at Jackson as he passed. Jackson loved living on Hackberry Street. It was not as elegant as Poplar Street, but still quite respectable, with neat homes and friendly neighbors. He waved at the Marlow sisters, who were sitting on their front porch drinking coffee.

The fact was that Jackson, for all his former ambitions to be a big-city cop, loved living here in Post Oak. He enjoyed the slow pace of his hometown. Post Oak had enjoyed a flurry of activity during the East Texas oil boom of the thirties, when oil was discovered under the old Jennerette farm. New people started coming to town, hustlers and speculators, roughnecks and drillers. There was excitement in the air, and everybody expected to be rich beyond their dreams within the year. For a few years, the promise of easy money had lifted the spirits of the Depression-weary local folks.

Lease hounds had occupied every street corner on Saturday afternoons, promising fortunes to farmers if they would only sign a lease on their mineral rights. And farmers were only too willing to sign for pennies on the acre. A few locals made money. Most had had to stand by and watch as their pastures and fields were cut into rutty roads leading to noisy, stinking drilling rigs that spewed out foul-smelling gas and not much more. Still, for a time little Post Oak had basked in a dream, before the oil dried up and the town settled back into sun-baked inertia.

Jackson turned at the end of his block, where residential gave way to commercial. He walked past the Wag-n-Bag and crossed the street to Main. He walked past the Wagon Wheel Café, which was closed for renovation, the hardware store, Odds & Ends Antiques, and Minton's Rexall. He walked down a side street and up the sidewalk to the courthouse.

When he pushed open the door to his office, he found Edna typing furiously. A frown creased her brow.

"What are you working on?" he asked.

"The Cramer divorce. I don't know why the hell she didn't dump him long ago. That fool has been beating up on her for twenty years."

"I know," Jackson said. "Well, she's doing it now. She wants to come in at one and sign. That way, we can get him served before night."

"She staying over at her sister's place?"

"Yeah, but keep it quiet. She doesn't want him to know where she is."

"Looks to me like that'd be the first place he'd look."

"Yeah, well, she's got a restraining order."

"And her brother-in-law, old Moose, is built like a two-ton truck. I know I wouldn't want to cross him."

"Any calls?" Jackson paused at the door to his office.

"Just the sheriff." She didn't look up from her computer screen.

Jackson sat down at his desk and dialed the sheriff's number.

"Judge, did you ever talk to Dickie and Brenda?"

"Not yet," Jackson said. "I'm planning to do that today."

"Well, it looks like we've got us a prime suspect — and it ain't neither one of them."

Jackson waited.

"It's the wife," Sheriff Gibbs said. "Her alibi don't check out at all."

"How's that?"

"Well, the bartender at the country club says the ladies left there at one — she says they played golf until four. And the lady down at Lucy's Boutique don't remember seein' her at all that day."

"Hmm," Jackson said. "Got an approximate time of death?"

"Doc says between four and six. He was still warm when Dickie and Brenda found him."

"Well," Jackson said, "I just have a feeling she didn't do it. Don't ask why. I'll report back to you when I talk to Dickie and Brenda."

"How come you feel that way, Judge? You said yourself that she acted mighty strange when you interviewed her."

"Yeah, I know. I'll talk to you later."

Jackson hung up the phone and got to work on the mountain of papers on his desk. He didn't look up until eleven, when Edna stuck her head in the door. "Horace Kinkaid's on the phone."

Jackson picked up the phone. "Hey, buddy," Horace said. "How about some lunch over at Dickie's place?"

The usual place for the lunch-and-coffee crowd, at least the male portion of it, was the Wagon Wheel, but now that Rip, the owner, had decided to close temporarily, business at the deli had picked up considerably.

"Okay. I'll meet you there in, what, thirty minutes?"

"Hell, Jackson. I'm already settin' at a table. Get your butt over here."

Jackson grinned and hung up the phone. Ten minutes later he pushed open the door of Dickie's place.

Horace, editor of the local newspaper, was pumping Dickie for information about the murder. He was holding a yellow legal pad and a ballpoint pen.

"Who you reckon did it, Dickson?" Horace had a tendency to make up nicknames for people.

"How should I know," Dickie replied. "I'm no detective. I just happened to be the unlucky SOB that had to find him." Dickie glanced around his place of business. All the tables were full, but Tiffany, his young waitress, had things under control. He sat down.

Jackson took a seat at the table and picked up a menu. He hid behind it to hide the big grin on his face. Horace's interview tactics were a source of constant amusement.

"How much blood did you see? Was the place a mess — like maybe old Tom fought for his life?"

Dickie turned a little green. "There wasn't hardly any blood. Just that one hole in his head."

"Well, how'd the killer get in? What about clues? Was the door lock broken?"

That got Jackson's attention. If there was no forced entry, then it must have been an inside job, and that didn't bode well for Mrs. Delgado. Of course, all the agents must have had keys. He would have to ask the sheriff about that. He cleared his throat, and Dickie looked at him for the first time.

Dickie was a pudgy man with wispy orange hair that he kept brushing away from his open and friendly face. "Sorry, Judge. I guess you want to order."

Jackson nodded. "I'll have the beef stew with corn bread muffins."

"Salad with that?"

Jackson shook his head. "You ordered?" he asked Horace.

"Yeah," Horace said. "I'm having the quiche with the fruit salad and the potato-and-leek soup." He glared at Jackson. "And don't you say a word."

"I wasn't going to," Jackson said. "So

what's the latest news off the presses?"

"The president's against the gays getting married," Horace growled, "and I don't give a shit. I want to know what's going on right here in Post Oak, and Dickie here ain't making it easy."

"I told you all I know," Dickie said. "All Brenda and I did was walk in and find him. Period." He got up and went to turn in Jackson's order.

Just then, Tiffany came over bearing Horace's food. "Quiche, fruit salad, and soup," she announced in a loud voice. Heads turned at other tables, and Jackson heard a titter coming from a group of ladies.

"Screw them," Horace said. "Where is it written that a man can't eat what he feels like?"

"Gender typing," Jackson said with a grin.

Horace dug into his soup. "Well, what do you know, Jackson? I heard you were out there that night."

"Not a lot," Jackson said. "Dickie went out to deliver food for their meeting and couldn't get in. Brenda came by and she had a key. They both found Tom Delgado, shot through the head."

"Suspects?"

"Nothing specific. The sheriff's working a couple of leads. That's all I can say now."

"The wife?"

Jackson shook his head. "That's all I can say."

"It's most always the wife or husband," Horace said with certainty.

"Hmm." Jackson inhaled the aroma of garlic as Tiffany set his stew in front of him.

Apparently Horace had given up, because he didn't mention the murder again. "What you reckon old Rip's doing over at the Wagon Wheel? He's keeping his mouth shut about it."

"Remodeling, is all I know," Jackson said. "It could use it."

"You got that right. And here he comes now."

Sure enough, the door opened and Wagon Wheel owner Rip Clark stepped into the room, looking decidedly uncomfortable.

"Hey, Rip," Horace called. "Casing the competition?"

Rip was looking with disbelief at the checked curtains at the window and the fresh flowers on all the tables.

"What is this, a damn whorehouse?" he asked, as he dropped down into a chair. He caught a glimpse of Horace's fruit salad and what might have been a smile crossed his craggy face. "What the hell is that?" he asked, pointing.

"It's a fruit salad, you clod," Horace said. "It's healthy. Not that you would know anything about that."

"How's the remodeling coming?" Jackson changed the subject.

"Slow," Rip said. "You can't get good help."

"Hey, Rip." Horace pushed his plate away. "Why don't you tell us what you're doing over there. I could come and take a few pictures, do a little write-up for the paper."

"Yeah — and charge me for an ad," Rip said. "You ain't fooling me with that line of bull again."

Horace laughed. "Smart boy," he said. "Well, I got to get back to work."

"Me, too," Rip said.

"You just got here," Jackson pointed out.

"I just seen you two fellers through that there frilly little window, and come in to see what the hell you was doing here."

"Well, now you know," Horace said. "You can go now."

Jackson took a bite of his stew, watching the door close behind Rip. It was delicious, filled with tender chunks of meat and baby onions, carrots, and potatoes in rich gravy. He tasted his corn bread. Equally good.

"How's Darla and the new baby?" he asked, before Horace could get back on the subject of the murder.

"Hell, I can't get a decent meal anymore. Ethel's always over there messing with him."

Darla was Horace and Ethel's daughter, and she had just had their first grandchild.

"I guess you don't like him much, then."

"Huh? Hell, yes, I like him. He's strong as an ox."

Jackson thought this was unlikely, since the baby was less than a month old.

"Got a grip on him like you wouldn't believe," Horace continued. "And a big head like mine. My mama said the reason she only had one kid was because, after she got my head outta there, she wasn't ever going through that again. 'Course Darla had little Jackie by cesarean. But, I was telling you how strong he is. Sunday, they came over to the house, and I had him on my lap. Well, that little peckerwood got a grip on both my fingers so tight I just lifted him right up off my lap. He held on like a little monkey."

"That right?" Jackson was wondering whether it had been a good thing to ask about little Jackie.

"Well, sir, my wife let out a scream, and Darla came running over and snatched him out of my lap. You'd have thought I was killing the kid. They said I could pull his arms out of their sockets. Hell, he don't weigh more than a mouse."

Jackson was spared any more stories when Dickie came over to the table, bringing their checks. "What was Rip doing here? He's never put a foot in here before."

"Checking out his competition, I guess." Jackson echoed Horace's assessment. "Got a minute? I'd like to ask you a few questions."

"Well, I got to be getting' on back," Horace said. "It's a cinch I'm not going to learn anything around here."

"Come on back to my office." Dickie led Jackson to a small office dominated by a huge rolltop desk. He removed a stack of papers from a chair and offered it to Jackson, while he took a seat at the desk. He picked up a purple toothpick and clamped it between his teeth.

Jackson grinned. "You're the second one I've seen chewing on one of those things," he said.

"I'm trying to quit smoking," Dickie said. He took the toothpick out and stuck it behind his ear. "It's not helping. Now what can I do for you, Judge?"

"Just a couple of questions," Jackson said. "No big deal."

Dickie's open face registered concern.

"You don't suspect me, do you, Judge."

"God, no," Jackson said. "When there's been a murder, we have to question everybody." He noted the quizzical expression on Dickie's face. "I'm just helping the sheriff out," he explained.

"Any way I can help, I want to." Dickie waited for Jackson's questions.

"Well, let's just start with a little background on you. I've got to admit that I don't know much about you. How did you wind up in Post Oak?"

"Fair question," Dickie said, "especially since I was born and raised in San Francisco." He looked at Jackson for a reaction, and when he got none, went on. "I've loved cooking and being around food all my life. Don't ask why. It's just always interested me. When I graduated high school, my parents were disappointed when I decided to go to culinary school instead of college." He picked up a pencil and tapped it against the back of his hand. "After I graduated, I worked in some of the best eating places in the city. Learned a lot."

Jackson nodded. "Guess so." He had asked a simple question, but now it looked like he was in for Dickie's complete life history.

"My dad was a rich man. He had big

plans for me and my brother to go into the family business. I was a disappointment to him." He paused for a long time, thinking. "But I was happy doing what I loved, and at the time, that was all that mattered to me. I was selfish, I guess. You see, I had opened a little bistro in San Francisco. It went over pretty good, but I didn't know anything about business. I lost it because of that. My dad disowned me and cut me out of his will. He told me I would never be welcome in his home again. It broke my mother's heart, and I'll never forgive him for that. I need a glass of water." Dickie got up and went out front, returning with two glasses of ice water. He took a sip of his and continued. "I got married, but my wife left me when the business failed. I got out of Dodge, as they say, and came to Texas." He held out his hands, palms up. "And as they say, the rest is history."

Jackson crossed his legs. "Why Post Oak?"

"Chance, really. I wanted to come south, and Texas had always intrigued me. I was traveling through, just looking around for a likely spot, and I happened into the Wagon Wheel." He laughed. "When I saw the swill old Rip puts out, I thought, this is the place for me." He grinned. "Make sense?"

"Yep," Jackson said. "What did you know

about Tom Delgado?"

"About the same as everybody else, I guess. He was a successful real estate broker — with a rich wife. That never hurts, you know."

"Had you ever done business with him before?"

"Once," Dickie said. "I catered his Christmas party last year."

Jackson stood. "Thanks." He turned to go, and then turned back. "What about Brenda Barns? Know anything about her?"

"Just know who she is," Dickie said. "She'd been in here maybe two or three times."

"So you wouldn't know how to get in touch with her."

"Seems like you could just go to her office — oh, yeah, I forgot. I guess her office isn't open. Wait. I might be able to help you."

He followed Jackson out and moved to the cash register. "We let people leave their business cards under the glass here." He indicated the glass-topped counter. "Yeah, here it is. She left hers. I knew I remembered it." He retrieved the card and handed it to Jackson. "There. She's got her home number and cell phone on it."

"Thanks. That helps a lot." Jackson pocketed the card and went out the door.

Back at his office, Jackson found Edna sitting at her desk eating a sandwich.

"Florice Cramer's coming in at one. Right?"

She nodded.

"Can you get her to sign the divorce petition and then take it over to the district clerk's office?"

"Jackson, haven't I done that a thousand times? Shit, I could get the damn divorce for her if I only had a license."

Jackson grinned. "You could, at that. Okay, I'm going to try to interview Brenda Barns. As soon as you get the thing filed, I want you to take a copy to the sheriff and tell him I want old Billy Wayne served before dark. Got it?"

Edna finished her sandwich and wadded up the waxed paper it had been wrapped in. "Go on, Jackson. I don't need you."

"Gotta make a call first," Jackson said, closing the door to his office.

CHAPTER FOUR

Jackson sat at his desk and took out Brenda's card. He first tried her home number and, getting no answer, dialed the cell phone. She picked up immediately. In a few words, Jackson stated his purpose.

"I'm on my way out to the lake to meet a client," Brenda said. "He's not supposed to be there until four. I was going out early to walk through the house. I've never shown it before."

"Well, is there another time . . . ?"

"Let me think," she said. "Tell you what, Judge. If you can meet me out at Apache Lodge ASAP we can chat a few minutes before I have to go."

"I'm on my way." Jackson hung up the phone and quickly walked home to get his car.

The Apache Lodge was a fishermen's camp set back in a grove of pines on the shore of Post Oak Lake. It consisted of several rustic cabins, a marina, a bait shop, and a restaurant-bar combination. Jackson pushed open the door to the bar and stood for a moment as his eyes adjusted to the dim light. The logs that the building was made of constituted the inside walls as well as the outside. Stuffed fish of all sizes and varieties were mounted on the walls, along with neon beer signs and a large calendar with a picture of a wide-mouth bass. There was a dance floor surrounded by tables, a bar, and a row of booths along the front window wall. Brenda was sitting in one of the booths sipping iced tea. She called out to him.

"Over here, Judge." He observed her as he approached the booth. She was polished as usual. She reminded Jackson of a shiny new black car that has just been driven through the car wash. Her hair was slicked back in a golden bun at her neck. She wore an expensive black pantsuit with a tailored gray blouse. Her makeup was heavy but skillfully applied. She smiled at Jackson.

"If you want something to drink, you have to go up to the bar to get it."

Jackson shook his head and slid into the booth. "I'm fine. Thanks for meeting me."

"What can I do for you?" she asked, and Jackson realized that she had the impression he was a prospect.

"Sorry if I've given you the wrong impression," he said. "I'm here to ask you a few questions about Tom. Helping out the sheriff."

Disappointment flashed across her face, but she quickly became solemn. "Terrible thing," she murmured. "I hardly slept the last two nights."

Jackson nodded and got down to business. "What I'd like to do is have you tell me a little about yourself, focusing on your relationship with Tom."

"Relationship?" She raised her eyebrows.

"Business, I mean."

"Oh. Well, let me see. I moved here from Texarkana. I'd just come out of a divorce and wanted a new start. I knew Post Oak was a hot market because of all the lakes around here, and I had heard of Tom Delgado. He was the hottest broker in three counties." She looked Jackson in the eye. "I was lucky to get on with him."

She gazed out the window for a minute, and Jackson saw that her face in repose was hard. It was only when she smiled that the anger went out of her eyes and she became somewhat beautiful. No wonder she smiled so often.

"How well did you know him?"

"As well as anybody could know Tom. He was all business. I don't think I ever had a personal conversation with him. Not that he couldn't be charming; he could. And he treated his agents well. It was just that you knew even when he was making small talk or asking about your health that his mind was always on the next sale." She smiled again. "I learned a lot from him." She paused. "It's impossible to believe that he's dead."

"How did you happen to come by the office when you did?"

"We were supposed to be having a meeting — Tri-County Realtors." She sipped her tea. "Well, I did arrive a little early because I had left some contracts in my desk. I was going to need them later that evening, because I was going to show the old Hall house on Convent Street. The people could only go at night."

Jackson listened, wondering why she had felt the need to share so much information with him.

"What time would you say you arrived?"

"About a quarter till. Six, you know. That's when the meeting was . . . supposed to be."

"And Dickie was already there?"

"Right."

72

"And you used your key to open the office?"

"That's right."

"Did all the agents have keys to the office?"

"I assume so. I wouldn't know." She drained her tea glass. "Judge, would you mind getting me a refill?"

"Of course not." Jackson went to get the tea and a glass for himself. When he came back, she was talking on her cell phone. She hung up as he slid her tea toward her.

"What do you know about Mrs. Delgado?" he asked.

"She's an empty-headed socialite," Brenda said. "Never had to work in her life."

Jackson raised an eyebrow but said nothing.

"Did they get along?"

"I wouldn't know," she said. "I really hardly know the woman."

Obviously, she regretted what she had just said. Jackson had a feeling there was more. He prodded gently. "It's a small town. Surely you came across her from time to time."

"I see her at the country club sometimes. And, of course, at Tom's big Christmas party at their house. She's just not a woman who makes an impression, if you know what

I mean."

"Well, you might have seen something, something that might have seemed insignificant at the time. It could be important now."

"Is she a suspect?"

"Not at this time." Jackson decided that if she thought he suspected Dossie, she might be more forthcoming. "Now, can you think of anything that might give us some insight into their relationship?"

"There was one time at the club," she said. "She'd had a few drinks, and Tom must have danced one time too many with someone, I've forgotten who, and she created a scene. Tom got her out of there really fast. I don't think many people noticed. I just happened to be seated at a table near the scene."

"What was your personal opinion of her?"

"Airhead," she shot back. "A complete and total airhead. I doubt if she had a thought about much more than hanging out with her Junior League friends, doing lunch, and playing golf and bridge. He worked like a dog to keep her in that big house with those expensive clothes — and servants." She thought a minute. "I wonder what he ever saw in her."

It would appear that Brenda didn't know about Dovie Delgado's money. He wondered if Tom had had anything to do with fostering that impression.

Brenda looked at the tiny Rolex on her wrist. "Sorry, Judge, I really have to go."

Jackson held up his hand. "Just one more thing," he said. "I really need to meet with the other agents in Tom's office. Any chance of that?"

"Sure," she said. "We have a tour scheduled for tomorrow morning. "We're meeting first at the community room at First State Bank — since our office is still off-limits. We'll have a short meeting and then go off to tour all our new listings." She picked up her tea glass, saw that it was empty, and set it back down. "Everybody should be there." She stood up. "Be there at eight."

"Thanks, I will. And thank you for your time."

She nodded and crossed the room, her heels clicking against the worn wooden floor. Jackson finished his tea and followed. Driving home, he had an uneasy feeling about her. She had given the impression of being open and honest, but somehow he got the feeling that she was holding something back. Her hostility toward Dovie Delgado was apparent. Was she having an affair with Tom? Possibly. Or maybe she just

75

wished she was. She was clearly driven by ambition, and just as clearly impressed by Tom Delgado. She had everything to lose and nothing to gain by his death.

Jackson stopped by the jail and spent an hour giving the sheriff a report on the two interviews.

"Don't sound like that amounts to a hill of beans," the sheriff said.

"I agree. But what do you expect? They're just the two who found him."

"That puts them on my suspects list any old day," Sheriff Gibbs said, leaning back in his squeaky swivel chair. "If they showed up and he was dead, I want to know why."

Jackson stood. "Well, they both had perfectly legit reasons for being there. Anyway, I'm going to meet with the agents tomorrow morning. I'll let you know what they have to say." He turned toward the door. "Now, I've got to go. Edna will have my hide."

Back at the courthouse, Edna was just shutting down the office.

"Going home early?"

"Jackson, would you look at your watch."

Jackson glanced at the clock on the wall and was surprised to see that it was five. "See you tomorrow," he said, hightailing it out of there before Edna could rag him about not knowing the time of day.

CHAPTER FIVE

Jackson stopped for gas at Cap Hilliard's Texaco. Cap was sitting in a chair out front, wiping his face with a red bandana.

"Hidy, Jackson," he called. "Feels like summertime already."

"Warm for March," Jackson agreed, fitting the gas nozzle into his tank. He walked over to Cap. "How's business?"

"Could be better if them damn oil prices would drop. I'm getting sick and tired of having folks come in here and cuss me out for it. Hell, I ain't got nothing to do with it."

"Bummer," Jackson commented.

"Hey, Jackson," Cap said. "It ain't none of my business, but isn't that little girl of yours friends with Ashley McBride?"

"Uh-huh." Jackson was watching the gas pump with his hand on the nozzle.

"I'd watch that if I was you."

"Why?"

"She come in here the other night with a car full of boys — and one of 'em was Mutt Tidwell's kid, Marvin."

"You're kidding!"

"Nope. That kid's poison, Judge. I don't like him or his gang anywhere around my place."

Jackson knew plenty about Marvin Tidwell. He had been in trouble with the law from the time he started junior high. If Ashley was running with his crowd, it wasn't good. Ashley was the daughter of his old friend Joe Junior McBride, who had been shot and killed a year ago. When you thought about how that had turned out, it was no wonder the child had problems. He'd talk to Patty about it the first chance he got.

"What were they doing?" he asked.

"Well, I can't say as to what they were doin'. I mean, they just drove up and pumped five gallons of gas in. The girl used the restroom and bought herself a Coke."

"Were there any other girls along — or just her?"

"Just her. That don't look good, Judge. I don't think so, do you?"

"I sure don't," Jackson said. "Well, thanks for the tip. I'll talk to Patty about this."

When Jackson walked into his kitchen he smelled the seductive aroma of Lutie's pot roast with its onion, garlic, tender beef, and peppery brown gravy. Lutie was mixing a batch of corn bread at the counter.

"You got time for a spell of relaxing tonight," she said.

"You mean you don't have any errands for me?" he teased.

"Go on in there," she said, waving her spoon at him, "before I think of some."

He stopped in the butler's pantry to mix himself a Scotch, and then headed for his den, taking the paper from the hall table as he went.

When he got there he found Patty sprawled in his easy chair watching MTV. He kissed her on the head. "How about letting your tired old daddy have his chair — and a little peace and quiet."

She looked up at him without a smile. "You never want to spend any time with me."

Jackson couldn't believe she was saying this. Most of the time he had to schedule an appointment with her just to go out to dinner or for a drive. To his way of thinking, she was the one who was too busy to spend time with him.

"Honey, I'm sorry. Want to talk now?"

"No. It's too late. You'd just be making yourself do it. I want you to ask me for once in your life! You love your work — and that Mandy — more than me."

"Wait a minute! Mandy? You're the one who wanted me to find a lady friend. You like Mandy, and she's crazy about you. What's going on here?"

Tears were now welling up in Patty's eyes.

"What is it, honey?" He took a step toward her.

"Don't touch me," she said. "You don't understand — you'll never understand." She went to the door, and then turned. "I don't want to talk to you right now." With that, she left, slamming the door. He could hear her feet pounding on the stairs to her room.

He stood stunned, facing the door. Finally he turned and sat down in his chair. This was a first. Patty had always been a happy girl, cheerful most of the time, and always ready to confide in him on the rare occasions when she wasn't happy. Maybe Lutie knew what was the matter. He went back into the kitchen.

"What's wrong with Patty?"

"Don't know," Lutie said. "She troubled, though. I heard her talkin' on the phone for close on to two hours when she got home from school. Then she just shut herself up in your den and don't come back out. I took her some cookies and milk, but she said she ain't hungry. When that girl ain't hungry for cookies and milk, they's something wrong."

"Well, keep your eyes and ears open."

"Yes, sir, I will."

Jackson shook his head and went back to the den. How was he supposed to know what to do with a teenaged girl? Mandy had always been able to help, but she was unavailable. Maybe not. He'd give calling her one more try. He lit a cigar and reached for the phone. To his surprise, she answered on the second ring.

"Mandy, good to hear your voice. I've missed you."

"You've called at a bad time, Jackson. Can I call you back later?"

"Mandy, this is important."

"Well, okay. What is it?"

"It's Patty. She's acting strange — and I don't know what to do."

"What has she done?"

He told her about Patty's uncharacteristic moodiness and about her running off to her room. "She said I don't want to spend time with her. You know that's not true."

"Jackson, she's going into adolescence. Their hormones start taking over, and they don't even know who they are half the time. Just be patient."

"It was more than that."

"It's the hormones," she said. "Trust me. Now, Jackson, I've really got to go. The . . . uh, the doctor's here to see my grandmother."

Jackson hung up the phone with a sense of foreboding. All was not well between Mandy and him — and he was damn well helpless to do anything about it. She was miles away in Victoria, and he was here. Worse, she was showing no signs of coming back. He sighed and sipped his Scotch. He tried to read the paper, but Patty's and Mandy's faces swam between his eyes and the print. He threw the paper on the floor and sat staring at the portrait of his grandfather Crain hanging over the mantle. Now, there was a man who always knew the right thing to do. Jackson wondered what he would have done in this situation.

The phone rang, and he reached for it, hoping it would be Mandy calling back. It was Lutie's niece, Cookie.

"Judge, I know it's late, and you're prob'ly tired, but we got a situation out here at Mrs.

Kruger's. Miss Roxanne asked me to call you."

"What's the matter?"

"Mrs. Kruger, she's not expected to last the night. And she's wanting to make a new will. She's real agitated, Judge. Will you come out here?"

"Well, yes. But I don't know how legal it will be. Is she rational?"

"Oh, yes, sir. She's got good sense."

"I'll be right out."

As Jackson drove to the Kruger place, he could see storm clouds building in the west. Spring storms were a common thing in this part of Texas. They could appear out of nowhere and rake the earth with powerful winds, hard rain, lightning, and, rarely, a tornado. Just as suddenly they would be gone. The grass always looked greener afterward. Local farmers had an explanation for it. They said the lightning put nitrogen into the soil. Jackson didn't know about that, but he was sure that the whole world turned brighter after the passage of one of these storms.

He turned the car up the tree-lined driveway that led to the sprawling Kruger ranch house just as a loud clap of thunder struck. He remembered Mrs. Kruger well. When she was still active, she was the personification of the legendary pioneer woman. Strong as a man, she had labored side by side her husband and the ranch hands, working cattle, feeding, mending fences. And yet, she could hold a barbecue or a ball that would be the talk of the town for weeks to come. After her husband died, she had managed the family's holdings with pragmatic thrift. The estate had prospered in her hands. He parked under an oak tree and, crossing the wide veranda, rang the doorbell. The woman who opened the door must have been Roxanne. Her hands on the doorknob were square, like a man's, and he could see traces of paint around the cuticles, although clearly an attempt had been made to scrub them clean. She was almost as tall as he, and her hair, blond and curly, was pulled back from her face with a rubber band. Strands had escaped and framed her face with ringlets. The face was thin, almost too thin, and the skin ivory and translucent. She had high cheekbones and a strong chin. Her lips were thin, but beautifully shaped. However, it was her intelligent eyes that drew his attention. They were set deep in her face and looked at him with curiosity and, oddly, a twinkle — as if she knew a secret that she would soon share with him. More than a little peculiar under the circumstances, Jackson thought.

"Come in," she said, and turned to lead him down a darkened hallway. "Mother's room is here." She held the door open for him.

Jackson didn't know what he expected to see, given the fact that he had been told that Mrs. Kruger was near death, perhaps a dimly lit room, the old woman so wasted by illness that she hardly made a bump on the bed. Labored breathing. The hush of death. These were the things Jackson expected. But what he saw when he entered that room was most definitely not anything of the kind. Mrs. Kruger was sitting up in bed, glasses on her nose, and complaining loudly.

"Where is that lawyer? I'm going to die before he gets here."

Jackson approached the bed.

"He's here, Mama," Roxanne said.

The old woman looked sharply at him. "Yes, Judge Crain. Thank you for coming. I want to make a change to my will. Only the problem is the will is in my safety deposit box at the bank."

"We can make a new will," Jackson said. "The new one will supersede the old one." He opened his briefcase and removed a simple will form. "Now, what do you want to do?"

"I want to leave the bulk of my estate to Roxie, including the house and ranch. That's in the old will. Now, I want to leave a nice trust for Cookie here, who has been an angel to me. I want it to be rock solid, so nobody can contest it." Her head fell back on the pillow, and she closed her eyes.

Jackson was making notes. "What do you want to leave for Cookie?"

Mrs. Kruger raised one hand and waved it toward Cookie and Roxanne. "Go," she said. The two left the room, closing the door softly behind them.

"I want to leave her five hundred thousand dollars, to be held in trust until the children start college. She will be allowed to draw the interest on a regular basis as income until that time."

"That's a lot of money," Jackson said, wondering if she really was in command of her senses.

"Nuts! There's plenty more than that. Roxie will never have to paint another picture, if she doesn't want to." She looked at him sharply. "I know what I'm doing, young man."

"Then so be it," Jackson said. "Five hundred thousand to Cookie, in trust, and the rest to Roxanne. Anything else?" He looked at the woman, who had closed her eyes. Her breathing was regular. Had she fallen asleep?

"I'm not asleep," she said. "Just resting. No, nothing else. I've already settled a little something on the hands."

Jackson wrote her bequests onto the will form and said, "You'll need witnesses. Obviously they can't be Roxanne or Cookie."

"Go and tell Roxie to bring in Juan and Alex. They are our ranch hands."

When the two men came in, embarrassed and looking at their feet, Jackson explained to them what they were there for and, placing the will in front of Mrs. Kruger, put the pen in her hand. She scrawled her signature across the line, and Jackson turned to the men.

"All we're asking you to do," he said, "is sign this, acknowledging that you witnessed Mrs. Kruger sign this document. Understand?"

Juan and Alex both nodded and added their names to the will. When Jackson had signed it himself and affixed his notary public seal, he folded it and held it in front of the woman.

"Where do you want to keep this?"

"Give it to Roxie." Her voice was now very

weak, as if the whole affair had tired her beyond belief. "And please go. I've got dying to do, and I choose to do it alone."

As she said that, the sky outside exploded with thunder, and rain came gushing down as if the sky had been ripped open by the last lightning strike.

Jackson went outside, where he found Roxanne seated in a chair in the hall. She stood and came toward him. He handed the will to her.

"You can't leave in this storm. Come and have some tea with me," she said, and turned toward the kitchen as if she had no doubt that he would follow.

He followed her down the darkened hall, thinking about Lutie's pot roast at home.

In contrast to the hall, the kitchen was large and well lit. A huge cookstove warmed the room just enough to take away the damp chill. A large table was in the center of the room covered with a brightly patterned oilcloth. He noticed that the room had been updated with all new appliances and granite countertops. Roxanne got out two glasses, filled them with ice, and motioned for Jackson to have a seat at the kitchen table. She went to the refrigerator and took out a pitcher filled with iced tea.

"It's sweet. I hope you like it that way."

Jackson nodded. She poured the glasses full and dropped into the chair opposite him with a sigh.

"Tough time," Jackson commented.

"The toughest." She sipped her tea. "Mother was a towering figure. It's hard to see her this way."

"She doesn't seem to be dying to me."

"Oh, that was an act. Her heart is gone and her lungs are filled with fluid. She only rallied for this will. She will be gone by morning."

"Shouldn't you be with her?"

"Cookie's in there. I needed this break. It's going to be a long night."

Jackson finished his tea and reached for the pitcher. He looked inquiringly at her, and she nodded, so he filled both glasses. "What are your plans?"

"Originally, I had planned to go back to New York as soon as I could get the estate settled. My plans may have changed."

"How's that?"

"I've started a series of sketches around the ranch. Landscapes. I want to finish those. When I get back to my studio, I'll turn them into paintings."

Jackson rested his elbows on the table and looked at her. "You can do that? Won't you have to be here to paint the pictures?"

She laughed softly. "No. Some people paint from life, but I rarely do. I prefer to work from sketches."

"But with just sketches, how will you remember the colors? How the shadows fall? I don't know a thing about art, but I would think you'd have to be there to paint it right."

"One of the first things an artist learns is how to see, really see, things as they are. When we are very young, our mind collects data about what things look like. That's why children's drawings all look so much alike, square houses with two windows, a door, and a chimney, lollipop trees. We lose our ability to look. An artist has to train herself to see what is there and not what her mind tells her should be there. Does that make any sense at all?"

Jackson shook his head and smiled ruefully.

She sipped her tea. "Well, I'll admit, it's complicated. It's just a matter of looking at things in a new way. And not only looking at the thing itself, but also the negative spaces around it. Furthermore, you have to be aware of where your light source is in relation to the object. That will be indicated in my sketches. You have to take into account the time of day. Is it sunny? Or cloudy? Summer, winter, fall, or spring? The sunlight is different in each of the seasons. Did you know that?"

Jackson shook his head again. He had no interest in how art was made, but he found that he had a growing interest in sitting here and listening to this woman talk. "Tell me more."

She sighed. "I don't think I can tell you all of it. It's just that art is a craft, and a craft has to be learned. There are ways to learn it, and if you fail to learn, no matter how talented you are, you'll remain only a dauber for the rest of your life."

"I see," Jackson said. "So, what you're saying is, if you know what you're doing, you can make paintings out of sketches." He grinned at her.

"Had enough, I see." She grinned back. "Well, I do tend to go on about it." She got to her feet. "I'd better go and be with Mother now."

The storm had passed by the time Jackson got back out to his car, and the moon was full. As he pulled out onto the farm road, he saw the moon reflected in the puddles, turning them into splashes of silver, and the droplets on the elderberry and sumac that grew wild in the ditches were quicksilver. He thought of Roxanne, who fascinated him. She was like those raindrops, beautiful, yet transient. The passion she felt for her work was white hot and, Jackson had to admit, he felt a stab of envy for that. He had none of that fire in the belly. Once he had had it, but that was only when he had thought about going into law enforcement work — and that was a long time ago. It wasn't that he hated his job. Nothing could be further from the truth. But, listening to Roxanne talk, well, maybe it was time for a change. Follow your bliss, somebody had said. Maybe . . . but, no. As he turned into his own driveway, the fantasy dissolved. His life was here in this town, raising his young daughter and doing exactly what he had been doing all his adult life.

CHAPTER SIX

Jackson was already cutting into his omelet when Patty came down to breakfast. Her eyes were red and swollen, and she looked like she had not slept well, if at all.

"What you want to eat?" Lutie asked.

"Cornflakes, I guess." She sat down at the table and did not look at Jackson.

He reached over and placed his hand on her arm. "Honey, something's wrong. Can't you tell your daddy? Maybe I can help."

"Nobody can help," she mumbled, and moved her arm away.

"Is it something at school?"

"No, it's not *something at school.* Daddy, will you please just leave me alone?"

They finished breakfast in silence, and Patty picked up her backpack and headed for the back door.

"Want a ride?" Jackson tried once again.

She shook her head and disappeared out the door. He heard her bicycle tires scrunch on the gravel of the driveway.

"What do you think?" he asked Lutie Fay.

"Don' know," she said. "Somethin', though."

"What should I do?"

"Wait 'til she decides to tell you, I reckon. Don't see no other way, she won't talk."

Jackson parked his car in the lot behind the bank and went into the community room, where he found a group of two men and three women standing around the coffee urn talking in low tones. Brenda Barns separated herself from the group and approached him.

"Everybody," she said, raising her voice. "You all know Judge Crain. He wants to ask us a few questions about poor Tom."

A tall man with gunmetal gray hair walked over and extended his hand. Jackson had the odd thought that this man looked like he had been created from spare parts. He was tall, towering over Jackson's six feet, and his head was thrust forward like a bird of prey. His features were even, and he might have been handsome if it hadn't been for his strange posture and abnormally small hands and feet. He was wearing a suit the color of his hair, with a black shirt and gray tie. "I'm Deke Slade," he said. "I'll be presiding over the meeting in Tom's place."

When the group was gathered around a long table, coffee cups in hand, Deke stood. "I know we're all wanting to get the tour over so we can make it to Tom's funeral," he said. "But the judge here has a few questions for us."

Jackson stood at the head of the table. "I know most of you," he said, "but if you don't mind, I'd like to just go around the table and get you to tell me your names and a little about yourself as it relates to Tom. Please understand that nobody is a suspect here. This is routine in a murder investigation. We talk to everybody who had any connection with the deceased." He turned to a woman on his left. "Angie, why don't you start?"

The woman stood and adjusted her skirt around her ample hips.

"I think you can remain seated," Jackson said with a smile.

Angie blushed and sat back down. "I'm Angie Sparks," she said. "I'm a single woman." Jackson squirmed as she looked provocatively at him, literally fluttering her eyelashes. "I've been working for Tom for eight months. Before that I was with Re-Max over in Marshall. As far as I knew, Tom was a great businessman and fair to his agents. I've more than doubled my commissions since I came to him. We're all going to miss him."

She looked at Jackson, who nodded. "Is there anything you can think of that might have been out of the ordinary lately. Any change in his demeaner? Any problems with the business?"

"No . . . only that he'd gotten religion. He talked a lot about God. That's all I can think of." She leaned toward him. "If I think of anything else, I'll be sure and call you."

"Good enough, then."

Brenda was sitting next to her. "We'll skip Brenda, since we've already talked."

The other agents glanced at one another curiously, but neither Jackson nor Brenda saw the need to enlighten them. A slender brunette, about forty, sat at the other end of the table. Jackson looked at her, and she jumped nervously

"Oh!" she said. "It's my turn." She laughed uneasily, and her hands shook as she fluttered them around her face. "Well, I'm Lindy . . . Lindy Hodge. I just do this part-time to have something to do. I'm a housewife with two teenaged kids who take up most of my time."

"And Tom?" Jackson prompted.

"Oh, yes. Well, I met Tom at the country

club. We were dancing, and I told him I was bored." She blushed beet red. "He suggested that I study for my real estate license and join his staff." She sat up a little straighter. "It's the best thing I ever did for myself. I haven't made many sales, but I'm learning . . . or was." She brushed a tear from her eye. "What are we going to do without Tom?"

"We'll just go on," Deke, who was next, said. "I have a broker's license. When the time is right, we'll go to Dovie and ask if we can continue to use the office, paying a fair amount of rent, of course. If not, we'll find another place."

Jackson interrupted. "Could you tell me a little about yourself?"

"Of course," Deke said. "I've known Tom for quite a while. We were business associates in Dallas. When Tom opened his business here, he contacted me with the offer of a job." He opened his hands in front of him. "That's it."

"So, I assume you got along well?"

"Like crackers and cheese," Slade said. "Never a cross word between us."

The last agent was a man Jackson knew well, Fred Moll, who also ran an insurance business on Main Street.

"What about you, Fred?" Jackson said.

"Met Tom when he first came to town. Wrote the policy on his house." Fred spoke in shorthand. "Never socialized. Strictly business between us. Made a nice living on the side selling real estate."

"Okay." Jackson got up. "Thank you all for your help."

As he was going to his car, he heard his name called. It was Angie Sparks. She caught up with him, and then looked back at the building.

"Judge," she said, "I wouldn't want anybody to know I told you this, but Deke wasn't exactly telling the truth in there."

"In what way?"

"The way he said he and Tom got along? That wasn't the truth. I heard them having a heck of a fight only last week. I was sitting at my desk in the outer office, and I guess nobody knew I was there. Anyway, Deke came storming out of Tom's office and, I'm telling you the truth, I've never seen a man's face so red." She looked back at the building again. "Lord, I hope he didn't see me talking to you."

"I don't think he did," Jackson said. "I saw him leave by the back door as I went out the front. May I call you, if I need more information?"

"Sure." She dug into her purse and

handed him a card. "By the way, Judge Crain, are you a married man?"

Jackson shook his head.

"Then you must come over for a drink sometime. I'll just give you a ring. Bye!"

She turned and walked back to the building on short, chubby legs.

At his office Jackson put away his notes from the meeting. He would go over them later. Right now he had something more important on his mind. He sat at his desk and thought about Patty. There was nothing he hated more than feeling helpless — and helpless was exactly how he felt now. There must be something he could do. He needed to take action, even if it was wrong, just to delude himself into the notion that he was working on the problem. Maybe he would call Mrs. Pullen, Patty's homeroom teacher. He was reaching for the phone when Edna stuck her head through the door.

"Jackson, aren't you going to Tom Delgado's funeral?"

Jackson looked at his watch. "Damn, I forgot."

"It's at ten."

"I'm on my way." He shrugged into his suit coat and headed out the door.

The sanctuary at the Methodist church

was full, and folding chairs had been brought in and placed around the edges of the pews. Jackson found a seat in the rear. He watched as the funeral director escorted Dovie Delgado to the front pew. They were followed by another woman, who Jackson suspected was Dovie's sister. The family resemblance was obvious. Since neither Tom nor Dovie had children, or apparently any more relatives who cared enough to attend, these two sat alone in the front pew.

Now the coffin was being wheeled down the aisle covered with a floral pall that must have cost plenty. It was made entirely of white orchids. Was there an element of guilt in that? Jackson knew that the sheriff, who was sitting two rows in front of him, would think so.

Brother Peterson, the minister, stood up and welcomed the crowd. He then launched into a lengthy prayer heavy with flowery phrases and pious platitudes. Jackson did not care much for this preacher, who spoke with piety but was conspicuously absent when local charities asked for his help.

When the prayer finally ended, the preacher folded his hands together on the lectern. "My friends, we are all here to honor the memory of a good man, Thomas Miguel Delgado. And we are privileged to have a renowned preacher and defender of the gospel to deliver the eulogy. Ladies and gentlemen, may I present the Reverend Mary Dobbs McDermott."

Jackson heard a gasp coming form Dovie Delgado. She half stood. "Who . . . ?"

Her sister tugged at her arm until she sat back down. The two women put their heads together and held a whispered conversation, and Mary Dobbs McDermott made her entrance.

She appeared from behind curtains that framed the large pipe organ. Her arms were outstretched, and she wore a flowing white robe edged with bands of gold. Her hair was silvery blond and worn in a bun at her neck. She was exceptionally tall.

The congregation let out a gasp as she strode to the pulpit. Her voice filled the church, sending thrills through the hearts of the less cynical. Jackson's first thought was: Damn, she's one hell of a showman!

Her eulogy matched her entrance. Now her voice was soft, almost a whisper, next it filled the church to the rafters. One moment she was bringing the audience to tears of loss, the next to titters of self-conscious laughter as she told some amusing story about Tom. She ended with a wave of the flag, stirring the audience with a heroic tale of Tom's valor on the battlefields of Vietnam. "He loved his country and his god, and we shall count ourselves lucky to have known such a man."

Jackson looked around him. It had been hokey beyond belief, but as he looked around, he could see that he was apparently the only one who saw through it. Then his eye fell on Dickie Deaver, and he knew that at least someone else had not been taken in. Dickie's face was impassive as he watched the lady preacher precede the casket down the aisle.

Dovie stood with Brother Peterson at the entrance, greeting each mourner as they exited the church. Her eyes were red-rimmed. Obviously, she had come out of her strange state of denial. When Jackson's turn came, Dovie leaned forward and whispered in his ear.

"Judge, I want you to meet my sister, Vangie."

Jackson smiled and shook the woman's hand. Dovie continued, "Will you come to the house after the graveside and enjoy the funeral luncheon with us?"

"No, I . . ."

She gripped his arm. "Please," she hissed.

Jackson looked down at her, surprised.

"There's a reason." She was talking rapidly, as the line behind Jackson got longer. "Curtis Gilmer was Tom's lawyer. He will be reading the will. I want you there to make sure everything is . . . done right."

"Curtis is a good man."

"Please!" She spoke out loud this time, and heads turned toward them.

"I'll be there." Jackson pulled away from her and beat a hasty retreat.

He decided to skip the graveside ceremony and went back to his office. He wanted to telephone Mrs. Pullen at school. He didn't really expect to talk to her immediately, since school was in session, but he would leave a message at the principal's office. As it happened, the teacher was on her break and could talk after all. Jackson outlined the problem at home.

"Do you know anything about it?"

"Well, I've been a little concerned about her myself. I'm not sure, and please keep this to yourself, but I think it has something to do with Ashley McBride."

"How so?"

"As you know, Patty and Ashley are quite close."

"I know," Jackson said. "They're best friends."

"Well, Ashley's been having some problems lately. I won't go into that, but I've just got a feeling Patty's mood has something to do with that. As for her grades, they're fine. Patty is one of my brightest students."

"Thanks," Jackson said. "And thanks for the information. I'll look into it."

When he hung up, he dialed Vanessa and Steve Largent's number. They had taken Ashley in after the tragic loss of her parents.

"We know," Vanessa said. "Something's wrong, and Ashley won't tell us a thing. I'm worried, Jackson."

Her husband, Steve, was on the extension. "Maybe we three should meet and talk this over."

"Good idea," Jackson said. "I could sure use some support here — and advice."

"Steve's got plenty of that last," Vanessa said, laughing softly. "He's still a preacher at heart and will be 'til he dies. He just loves to give out advice. Don't you, honey?"

Jackson heard Steve chuckle and hang up the phone. With Vanessa, he made arrangements to meet as soon as possible at the Rice mansion, where the Largents lived with an ever-changing number of foster children.

Jackson looked at his watch. It must be about time for the graveside service to be over. He once again put on his suit coat and went into the outer office.

"I'm going to the Delgado place," he told Edna.

"What for? You weren't ever friends with those folks."

"I know. Dovie wants me there for her own reasons."

"What reasons?" Edna was a great one for asking questions.

"I'll tell you later," Jackson said.

"Wait." Edna whirled around in her stenographer's chair. "Roxanne Kruger came in this morning."

Jackson felt a prick of disappointment at having missed her. "What did she want?"

"The old lady died. She brought in the will."

"Okay. I'll deal with that in the morning."

The parking lot at Del-Max Realty was full, and cars were parked in the driveway as well. Jackson parked on the street and went up the wide front steps to the door. It opened before he could ring the bell. Lutie's cousin, Fayrene, stood there wearing a white uniform

"Mrs. Delgado need you in the library," she said. "Follow me, please."

"Thank you, Fayrene." He followed her down the wide hall to a door on the left. He could hear a tumult of voices combined with the clinking of glasses from the living room on the opposite side of the hall.

When he entered the library, Curtis Gilmer was seated at the desk. Dovie and her sister were seated in wingback chairs in front of the desk. He was surprised to see Mary Dobbs McDermott perched on the leather sofa against the wall. She sat primly, with her hands folded in her lap, but she could not hide the slight smile that danced across her face and disappeared as quickly as it had come. She looks like the cat that ate the canary, Jackson thought.

"Jackson, come in," Curtis said. "Dovie specifically wanted you here before we read the will."

Jackson crossed the room and shook hands with Curtis, nodded to the ladies, and took a seat in a straight chair behind the sisters. He wasn't sure why he was here, and he intended to keep a low profile until he found out.

"All right then, let's get started," Curtis said. He opened the heavy white folder that held the will. "Why don't I just read it in its entirety, and then you can ask questions as you wish?"

Curtis hurried past the required legal language of the opening paragraphs and got quickly to the bequests. "I leave my community estate of the house and grounds at 310 Poplar Street to my beloved wife, Dovalene Wynn Delgado, to do with as she shall see fit. The remainder of the property I may die possessed of shall go to the Reverend Mary Dobbs McDermott to be used at her discretion in the furtherance of her great ministry in spreading the Word of the Lord to all His people."

Curtis reddened and looked at Jackson. "He insisted on that wording," he said.

Jackson nodded. He looked at Dovie. She had taken a handkerchief from her lap and was dabbing at her eyes. Her sister had leaned toward her and was speaking softly to her. He looked at Mary Dobbs McDermott. She wasn't even trying to hide her pleasure now. She smiled broadly and moved over to Dovie's side.

"Shall we have a prayer together?"

Dovie looked up at her with hatred. Suddenly she stood up and faced the woman. "You bitch!" she screamed. "You stole my husband, and now you've stolen my inheritance." She stood panting and staring at the woman, who regarded her with what could only be described as contempt. "Get out of my house. Get out now! This place is still mine, at least. You are a bible-spouting hypocrite and a seducer of other women's husbands. You should rot in hell for this — and I hope you do!"

She lunged at Mary Dobbs McDermott and grabbed her hair with both hands. Jackson stepped forward and put his arms around her, pulling her off the lady preacher. Dovie went limp in his arms, and Vangie quickly took her by the arm and led her to a chair at the opposite side of the room.

The lady preacher smoothed her hair with both hands and faced Curtis Gilmer. "I will be in touch," she said coolly and left the room, closing the door quietly behind her.

"I'm sorry, Dovie," Curtis said. "I tried to dissuade him, but he was adamant. That woman had quite a hold on him."

"I know." Dovie was calm again. "He thought she had brought him eternal salvation — and he had just about given up hope of that. Of course, I knew she was a complete fraud. I had her investigated." She wadded the handkerchief in her lap. "Would you believe, she was a showgirl in Las Vegas before she took up preaching? Traded one kind of show business for another, if you ask me. But when I tried to explain that to Tom, he said it was the devil talking through me. The devil! His own wife!" She collapsed into tears again. "It's not the money," she sobbed. "I have plenty of my own. It's just that . . . how could he . . . do that to me?" She buried her head in her sister's breast, and Vangie led her from the room.

Jackson and Curtis Gilmer walked out to their cars together.

"This is one will that I wish I could wash my hands of," Curtis said.

Jackson grinned. "Glad it's you and not me, buddy," he said. "I've got a feeling that McDermott woman is going to make you earn every dime of your fee."

CHAPTER SEVEN

When he left the Delgado home, Jackson realized he was starved. He looked at his watch and saw that it was two. He stopped in at Dickie's Deli for a sandwich. Dickie stood behind the counter, the usual purple toothpick behind his ear. All the tables were empty except one, at which a pair of ladies Jackson didn't know were sipping tea and eating scones in the corner.

"Judge!" Dickie smiled pleasantly. "What can I do for you?"

Jackson walked over to the glass case and examined its contents. "Let me have a large éclair and one cream-filled donut," he said, "to go. I missed my lunch today."

"Let me make you a sandwich," Dickie said. "It won't take a minute — and it'll be a damn sight more healthy."

But Jackson could taste the whipped cream oozing out of that éclair already. "No, thanks. I've already got my mouth set for those." He pointed to the éclairs.

"Didn't see you at the funeral today," Dickie said, as he sacked the treats.

"I was there — three rows behind you, across the aisle."

"What did you think of that lady preacher?"

"About the same as you," Jackson said grinning. "I saw the look on your face."

"Yep." Dickie handed Jackson the bag. "That woman's phony as a mule with a foal. How 'bout a cup of coffee to wash these down with — on the house."

"Thanks, I will." Jackson accepted the paper cup Dickie handed him.

By the time Jackson had finished the last of his food, he was pulling into his parking space at the courthouse. In his office, Edna was standing at the fax machine receiving a fax. She turned when he came in.

"How'd it go out at Dovie's?"

"He left almost everything to Mary Dobbs McDermott." Jackson came up behind her to read the fax she was holding. It was a menu from the Apple Barn, a restaurant in Center Point.

"I hate these goddamn things," Edna said. "We get them all the time. Who do they think they are, wasting our paper like that?"

Jackson took the menu and tossed it into

the trash. "Anything I need to be doing?"

Edna sat back down in her chair and looked up at him. "Jimmilee Pilgrim came in. She's having trouble with her house insurance. I made her an appointment for the morning at ten."

"Good. I'm going over to talk to the sheriff. Be back in an hour."

Edna looked at her watch. "Don't expect to see me then. It's four fifteen right now."

Jackson had his hand on the doorknob when the phone rang. He waited while Edna answered.

"He's on his way over there right now, Sheriff," she said.

Jackson nodded and walked briskly across the parking lot to the jail. The door opened before he could knock. It was the sheriff's wife, Norma Jean.

"Come on in, Judge. Lennie's got a big old problem on his hands."

Jackson followed her into the sheriff's office and found Sheriff Gibbs talking on the phone. As usual, Dooley was slouched in a chair trimming his nails with a pocketknife.

"Here's the judge now," the sheriff said into the phone. "I'll call you back later."

Jackson took a seat. "What's going on?"

"That was the DA. He wants me to go out and arrest Dovie Delgado right now."

Jackson didn't know the DA very well. He was a young lawyer just out of law school, Tad Padgett. Jackson guessed he was wanting to make a name for himself handling a case in which a prominent family was involved.

"Bad mistake," Jackson said.

"That's what I think, too." Sheriff Gibbs unwrapped a stick of gum and put it in his mouth. He held the pack out to Jackson, who shook his head.

"Tryin' to quit smoking," he said. "Chewing this damn gum ain't helping."

"So, what are you going to do?" Jackson asked.

"Try to put him off as long as I can. She can be more good for us running around loose than locked up in jail. 'Sides, she'd be bonded out by nightfall."

Jackson shook his head. "There's no bond for capital murder."

The sheriff gripped the arms of his chair. "Shit, I forgot. That would mean we'd have to keep that rich lady in here until trial. Judge, we got all kinds comin' in and out of there. It ain't no place for a lady."

"I agree," Jackson said.

"Still and all," Gibbs said, "her story don't jibe — and I ran a check on Tom's bank records. He's been sending a shitload of money to that preacher lady."

"He also left everything to her in his will," Jackson said, "except the house."

The sheriff looked shocked. "You're shittin' me!"

Jackson shook his head.

"How'd she take it?"

"The way any wife would, I imagine," Jackson said. "She was plenty upset."

"Well, you can't blame her for that. That don't mean she killed him, though. How 'bout those agents? Find out anything there?"

"Maybe." Jackson gave the sheriff a rundown on his meeting with the agents. He told him about what Angie had said about hearing Deke and Tom arguing. "I think this guy, Deke, is interesting," he said. "Might want to do a background check on him."

"Right. Judge, you reckon you could talk some sense into that young shave-tail DA? Maybe since we've got another possible perp, he'll back off Miss Dovie for a spell."

"Probably not, but I'll give it a shot." Jackson stood. "In fact, I'll step over to his office right now."

Jackson went back into the courthouse and up the elevator to the DA's office. The district offices were on the second floor, while the county offices occupied the first floor. He pushed open the outer door and entered the reception area. The DA's secretary, a polished young woman in her twenties, was typing with incredible speed on her computer keyboard. She turned when Jackson entered.

"Hi, Judge Crain," she said. "Bet you don't recognize me."

Jackson looked at her. Her face was perfectly made up, her blond hair cut short in a neat bob, and her feet shod in sheer nylons and expensive-looking shoes. Secretaries on the second floor must get better pay than those in the first, he thought with amusement. He looked again at her.

"Melanie Bacon," he said. "You're right. I didn't recognize you at first. You're all grown up."

Melanie had been a babysitter for Patty when she was younger. She had been efficient and trustworthy and had needed the money, as her widowed mother just managed to scratch by on the small salary she made working at the grocery store.

"How's Patty?"

"Great," Jackson said. Now was not the time to discuss his concerns about his daughter. "Is Tad in?"

Melanie stood up. "I'll let him know you're here," she said.

She went into the inner office and closed the door. A few minutes later the door opened, and Tad Padgett came out, followed by his secretary, who took her seat and went back to working on the computer.

"Judge Crain." Tad put out his hand. "Glad to see you. Come on in." Tad was a slight man with thin blond hair that kept falling down over his eyes. He reminded Jackson of the boys who followed Patty around all the time, callow, but eager to please.

After shaking the younger man's hand, Jackson followed him into the office and took the seat the DA pointed to. Tad sat behind a desk that threatened to swallow him whole. With some effort, he reared back in his chair and swung his feet onto the desk.

"What's on your mind, Judge?"

"It's about the Delgado case," Jackson said. "None of my business, but I just talked to the sheriff, and he's telling me you've got an arrest warrant for Dovie Delgado."

Tad nodded, but a flash of uncertainty crossed his face.

"Is there a problem with that?" He looked squarely into Jackson's eyes.

"I think so," Jackson said, knowing there was a good chance that his interference

117

could cause this young lawyer to dig in his heels in defense of his decision to arrest Dovie.

"I'd like to hear your thoughts, Judge." Tad's face was open and genuinely interested.

Jackson nodded. "Here's the thing. As far as I know, what you have is a pretty weak circumstantial case against her. Her story doesn't check out. That gives her opportunity, no doubt about that. He'd been giving large sums to the lady preacher as well as spending way too much time with her. That would be motive in just about any woman's eyes — that is, if she was the murdering kind."

Tad nodded.

"Thing is," Jackson went on, "that's just about all you've got — that I know of. Got any hard evidence at all? Without that, you've got no case, and it could look real bad if you arrest her and have to release her. Make sense?"

To Jackson's surprise, Tad smiled and nodded. "I'm a politician, Judge. This job is a first step for me. My ambition is to be attorney general of this state, and after that, who knows?"

"And?"

"And, I'm not about to do anything stupid

to jeopardize that."

Jackson nodded and said nothing.

"Bottom line, I'll take your advice — for now. I understand you're quite the armchair detective yourself."

"I get interested."

"So, will you be helping the sheriff — and my office — on this one?"

Jackson nodded. "It's possible that Dovie did this, but my gut tells me otherwise. How about giving me a week to come up with another suspect?"

"Take all the time you need, Judge — within reason. We need to crack this one soon. The Dallas TV guys called me up yesterday. They've got wind of it, and the connection to Mary Dobbs McDermott. That lady is a bog frog in the Metroplex pond, apparantly. Publicity can be good — or it can turn around and kick you in the ass. Think JonBenet Ramsey."

"I met with the agents from Tom's office this morning," Jackson said. "What do you know about Deke Slade?"

"Not a thing," Tad answered. "Seen him around, of course. The guy's hard to miss. He plays golf at the club every Sunday afternoon, and he's been in a few of our tournaments. The guy's a pretty good golfer, if you can believe it."

"Um-hmm."

Tad laughed. "But you ought to see his swing. He looks like a gorilla out there, but his ball always goes right down the middle of the fairway."

Jackson got up to go. "Well, that doesn't make him a suspect. But he's the only one who knew Tom before he came here, so I think we need to check him out."

"Right," Tad said. "Okay, I'll hold off on Dossie for a while. See what you can do."

"I'll keep you informed," he said, as he left the room.

When he got back to his office, Edna had left, but he found several notes on his desk. He riffled through them and found messages about four phone calls that could wait until morning. The fifth could not wait. Jackson read: "Lutie Fay called. She said to tell you to go out to that farm stand on Highway 10 and pick up a mess of green beans for tomorrow and a basket of blueberries for supper tonight. She said get some tomatoes if they looked like good ones."

Jackson pocketed the note and left, locking the office behind him. He got into his car and drove out Highway 10 toward Ben Onderdunk's place. Ben was a frugal German, and one of the finest truck farmers in the area. He gave the farm stand to his wife and kids to earn their spending money. Jackson parked in front of the place, admiring the neat rows of tomatoes, squash, corn, and onions. Bushel baskets overflowed with cream peas, crowder peas, purple hulls, black-eyes, butter beans, and pole beans.

When Jackson walked up, Mrs. Onderdunk was helping another customer. Young Angie approached him. "Hey, Judge, we got some fine, fresh pattypan squash today."

Angie was in Patty's class in school and Jackson knew her well.

"I'm on a mission, Angie," Jackson said. "Lutie Fay sent me after green beans, blueberries, and tomatoes, if you've got some good ripe ones."

Angie picked up a paper sack. "You want pole beans or Kentucky Wonders?"

"Now you've got me. Kentucky Wonders, I guess.

"How many, do you reckon?"

"Oh, uh, enough for Patty and Lutie and me, I guess."

Angie picked up a two-pound basket and dumped its contents into the sack. "This'll do, and some left over for soup. The blueberries aren't in yet, but we got some mighty fine strawberries."

Jackson much preferred strawberries. "I'll

take that bunch right there." He pointed.

Angie picked up another basket and dumped its contents into another sack.

"Why, it's Jackson Crain."

Jackson turned and saw that the customer Mrs. Onderdunk had been helping was Roxanne Kruger. He looked at her with pleasure.

"How are you?"

"Better," she said. "Cookie is helping me deal with Mother's things."

"I'm glad. That's not much fun." Jackson remembered how it had been after his wife died; he had not had the heart to go through her things for a full year, and then only when Mae Applewhite and some of the ladies from the church had offered to help.

"No," she said shortly. Jackson eyed her as she poked through a basket of cherry tomatoes, fingering the top ones out of the way so she could see what was underneath. Finally, she said, "I'll take these tomatoes and three pounds of the pattypan squash. Now, how do you cook these things?" She pointed to the squash.

Jackson laughed. "Do what I do. Give them to Cookie and ask her to cook them for you."

She smiled. "Buy you a Coke?"

"Sure, but it's on me." He walked over to

122

the cooler out front and bought two sodas. When he got back, she pointed to a bench in the shade of an apple tree and started walking toward it. Jackson followed, bemused at her take-charge manner. Having lived all his life around Southern women, who learned at their mothers' knees to take a backseat to the male of the species, he found this boldly assertive woman fascinating.

They sat for a while watching the sun go down behind the stand of trees across the road. Jackson looked at her. She wore a rumpled man's shirt tucked into well-worn jeans and cowboy boots. Her hair was pulled back from her face with some sort of comb, but most of it had escaped and hung haphazardly around her face and shoulders. Her nose was aquiline and dusted with a few pale freckles. Her mouth was small and the lips thin. Not a combination that should add up to great beauty, but on her, it worked. Maybe it was the directness of her gaze or her total lack of self-consciousness, or the regal way she carried herself. Jackson found himself comparing her to Mandy, whose features were full and sensual and her skin tan and smooth as a baby's. Even after a full day of work, Mandy managed to look as fresh and neat as when the day began. Her clothes were ironed within an inch of their lives. Her hair, black and glossy as a blackbird's wing, was never out of place. Once, during sex, Jackson had intentionally mussed her hair with his fingers just to see what it would look like. He never found out because her hand instinctively went up to smooth it. Roxanne's hair was all over the place, and he wondered how it would feel to run his fingers through it.

"So," he said," when do you think you'll be leaving?"

She finished her drink and crushed the can between her hands. "Not soon. I'm intrigued with the landscape around Post Oak County. Excited, really. I'm going to do a series of paintings and sketches. Enough for a show, I hope."

Jackson didn't know why that pleased him. "Can I see sometime?"

"Come out Saturday for lunch. We're having pattypan squash!"

"I'd be a fool to miss out on that," he said. "About noon?"

"Come earlier, and I'll show you what I've done so far. Then, after lunch, I'll take you out and show you the places I want to paint. Do you ride?"

"Yep. Eleven, then?"

She nodded.

He looked at his watch and stood up. Lutie would be wondering about her berries. "Got to go, or I'm in trouble," he said.

She waved as he made his way over the rough ground to his car. When he got home, he realized that he had left his bags of beans, tomatoes, and berries behind. Sheepishly, he turned the car around and went back to get them.

CHAPTER EIGHT

The next morning Jackson failed to hear his alarm and slept until almost eight. By the time he came down for breakfast, Patty had already left for school.

"She say she got to get there early to study in the library," Lutie Fay explained.

"How did she seem?"

" 'Bout the same. Don't say nothin'."

Jackson poured himself a mug of coffee and went to the phone. He dialed the Largents' number. Steve answered. "Hey, buddy. What's up?"

"Still worried about Patty. How's Ashley doing?"

"Moody. Won't talk. Van keeps saying it's just her age, but I don't buy that. A happy, good-natured girl doesn't change overnight, hormones or no."

"I agree," Jackson said. "How about I drop by after work and the three of us have that little secret powwow we talked about.

Is Ashley going to be around?"

"Thursday? Nope. Band practice after school."

"Then I'll see you about five." Jackson hung up the phone and returned to the table. He bolted down the omelet Lutie had put on his plate and drained his coffee. "Gotta go," he said. "I'll be a little late getting home. I'm meeting with the Largents tonight."

"I ain't got ears to hear?" Lutie Fay replied. "Supper be 'bout seven thirty, then."

Jackson looked at his watch. It was already nine, but he wasn't ready to go to the courthouse yet. He poured another cup of coffee and went out to the front porch to sit on the swing. He thought about Patty and wished with all his heart that his wife, Gretchen, were still alive. Gretchen would know what to do. A girl could talk to her mother. At least, he thought that was so.

As he sipped his coffee, his mind went back to Gretchen. Strange, he hadn't thought much about her in over a year. Strange because they had meant so much to each other. He tried to picture her face, but it had become hazy with time. She had been a feisty little thing, he remembered that, full of laughter and energy, and the best joke teller in seven counties. She had loved Jackson and Patty more than life itself, and that had sustained her for a long time when she, at thirty-seven, was diagnosed with leukemia. Jackson smiled sadly at the thought of how valiently she had fought the disease, how brave she had been through the chemo treatments when her skin had turned the color of clay and her hair had fallen out in great clumps. She had laughed and cracked jokes almost to the very end. And she would know what to do about Patty. "Help me, Gretchen," he whispered. But, of course, there was no answer.

He got up and went back inside.

At the office, Jackson found Jimmilee Pilgrim waiting for him. She was a slight woman in her fifties, with fading red hair and freckles that covered her face, neck, and arms. Her blue eyes were so pale you could hardly distinguish the white from the iris. She was dressed in a polyester pantsuit, turquoise, worn with white tennis shoes.

"Come on in, Jimmilee," Jackson said. He indicated a chair for her and sat down behind his desk. "Now, Edna tells me you're having trouble with your insurance. That right?"

"Yessir, that's right, Judge. And what I

want to know is how come I've been paying them folks $176.50 every month, and they won't even fix my roof when it needs fixing." She pulled her chair closer to the desk. "You'll have to speak up, Judge. My hearing ain't what it used to be."

Jackson opened his mouth to speak, but Jimmilee wasn't finished yet.

"You see, ever since Danny died, I been wanting to sell out and move over to Shreveport, where my daughter lives, but I don't reckon I'll be able to sell that old place with the roof being what it is."

"So, you've already contacted the insurance company?" Jackson asked.

"About a million times." She pulled a wad of letters out of her handbag. "They always say the same thing: no."

"Maybe I'd better take a look at those," Jackson said.

She shoved the papers across the desk at him. "Look all you want to. But I reckon you're going to have to write a real mean letter to them before they're going to send me my rightful money."

Jackson separated the letters Jimmilee had written from the company's responses, and then sorted them by date. He shoved the policy to the side. As he read, it began to dawn on him just what the problem was.

Finally, he looked at her. "Now, just how was your roof damaged?"

"Old age, that's how. Heck, Judge, that roof's been on that old house since right after they shot Kennedy. I remember because they was showing his funeral on TV while them fellers were banging away over my head. Now it's leaking like a sieve."

Jackson cleared his throat and wondered how he was going to convince this woman of something she did not want to believe. He had been down this road before. Clients invariably found it difficult to understand things that did not suit them.

"You see, Jimmilee," Jackson said. "You have to have had actual damage to your roof before the insurance is going to pay. They don't pay for normal wear and tear."

"My roof's leaking and I got buckets settin' around everywhere. It's done already leaked on my mama's crocheted bedspread and the rug she hooked with her own two hands. They're ruin't. I call that damages."

Jackson looked at the policy. "Your deductible is thousand dollars. I doubt if those two things will come to that. Why didn't you just get the roof fixed when it first started leaking?"

"Because Danny Joe Pilgrim was tight as paint on a wall, that's why. I used to tell him all the time we needed to get that roof fixed, but no, he'd just get up there with a hammer and put a piece of tin over the leak." She looked forlorn. "What am I supposed to do, then? I can't sell the house like it is — and I sure ain't got the money to fix that roof."

"Exactly where is your house?" Jackson asked.

"It's out on Chinkypin Road. Right near that new lake they put in."

"Uh-huh. Isn't that where the new power plant is going in?"

"I reckon. Danny used to get letters from them folks wantin' to buy the place all the time, but he just throwed them in the trash. That place belonged to his mama and daddy, and he wasn't about to let them tear it down to put a road in." Suddenly her face brightened. "Hey, Judge, you reckon they're still interested? It's been the better part of a year since we got one of them letters."

"Let's find out." Jackson picked up the phone and dialed Curtis Gilmer's number. When the other lawyer came on he asked, "What's going on with Tom Delgado's business? Is it shut down, or what?"

"No way," Curtis said. "Sister McDermott wanted it kept in operation. More money

131

for her, don't you know."

"You don't have much use for her, do you?"

"Nope. What's your interest, Jackson?"

Jackson told him about Jimmilee's problem.

"Call Deke Slade. He's the best there is — and I happen to know he's been dealing with that power company and their acquisitions."

"Thanks, I will," Jackson said.

"Hey, before you hang up, what's the deal on the investigation?"

Jackson glanced at Jimmilee, who was all ears, and swiveled his chair away from her. "They're looking at the wife," he said in a low voice.

"Ridiculous!" Curtis said. "If it was me, I'd zero in on the lady preacher. She had the most to gain."

"Yeah, well . . . thanks for the information."

After he hung up, Jackson looked up Deke Slade's phone number and wrote it on the back of one of his business cards. "You call this man. He can help. Forget about the insurance company for now. If the power company wants your place, they're going to tear down the house anyway."

"Judge, you're a wonder," she said. "And

don't worry none, I'm telling all my friends about you."

Jackson smiled as he shook her hand, imagining all the niggling problems he might find himself solving if Jimmilee sent in all her friends.

Jackson sat for a while, thinking about Mary Dobbs McDermott. Could she have been the one who shot Tom Delgado in cold blood? He wasn't naïve enough to think that a woman of God couldn't do such a thing; he just doubted that a person of her celebrity would jeopardize her position by committing the murder herself. Surely, she would hire it done. He leaned back in his chair and closed his eyes. Suddenly, a scene jumped into view. It was the day of the murder. He was driving back home from the county officers' meeting. Yes! She had passed him on the road, driving like a bat out of hell. He picked up the phone and dialed the DA's office.

Tad himself answered the phone. "Hey, Judge. I was just coming down to see you. You free now?"

"Come on over," Jackson said.

Moments later, the door opened, and Edna stuck her head in. "DA," she said.

Jackson motioned to her to send him in.

When Tad was seated in the clients chair

across from the desk, he said, "I'm afraid it's looking worse for Dovie Delgado, Judge. The sheriff's deputy found a snub-nosed .38 buried in the vegetable garden behind her house. She admitted it belonged to her. Said Tom had gotten it for her for protection when she traveled to Dallas to visit her family."

"Uh-huh. Any forensics?"

"No prints, wiped clean. We've sent it to the lab. If it matches the slug that killed Tom, well, I guess I'll have to bring her in."

"Not so fast," Jackson said. "Anybody could have buried it there."

Tad shifted in his seat. He wasn't any more enthusiastic about arresting Dovie Delgado than Jackson was. He had come to realize that he could end up looking like a fool if she turned up innocent.

"There's more. Her gardening gloves were covered with dirt."

Jackson sighed. "So . . . ?" He wasn't going to state the obvious: that they were *gardening gloves,* for Christ's sake.

"The maid said she never actually digs in the garden. They hire somebody for that. Mrs. Delgado uses the gloves when she goes out to cut flowers for the house. And besides — they were hidden under a watering can in the shed."

"Why wouldn't she just pitch them in the trash?"

Tad nodded. "I thought of that. All I can say is, she's a pretty ditzy woman, if you ask me."

Jackson buzzed for Edna, who immediately stuck her head through the door. "Could we get a couple of cold drinks in here?" Edna kept a small refrigerator in the copy room stocked with soft drinks. "I got colas and oranges," she said.

"I'll take an orange," Tad said grinning. "Haven't had one of those since I was a kid."

"Make that two." Jackson waited until Edna had closed the door before speaking. "What do you know about Mary Dobbs McDermott?"

"We interviewed her," Tad said. "Seems she was holding a trustees' meeting at that big church of hers when the murder took place."

Jackson waited while Edna brought the drinks in. He nodded his thanks. "Verified that?"

Tad reddened. "Not really. She's a preacher, you know."

"Well, what would you say if I told you I saw her speeding out of town on the evening of the murder?"

Tad set down his drink. "You're shittin' me."

Jackson shook his head, and then told the DA what had happened the night he returned from the county officers' meeting. "She ran me off the road," he finished. "I saw her license plate as she drove away."

"Dammit to hell," Tad exploded. "There's your reasonable doubt right there — and there goes my case."

"Maybe not," Jackson said. "We don't know Dovie didn't do it. I just want to snoop around a little more. Okay with you?"

Tad stood up. "Guess it'll have to be." He grinned ruefully. "Thanks for saving me from making one hell of a mistake."

Jackson followed him to the door. "I'll keep you posted. Any objection to my having a talk with Dovie?"

"None." Tad shook his hand and left.

Jackson returned to his desk and signed the pile of documents Edna had left there. He gathered up the files and took them to her.

"Set them over yonder on top of the file cabinet," Edna said. She looked at the clock on the wall. "Hey, Jackson, I know it's just now three, but would it be okay if I took off the rest of the afternoon?"

"Sure. But what's your hurry?"

She had her head under her desk searching for her handbag. "My hurry is," she said, emerging, "that the damn fool husband of mine is laid up on the couch with a bullet hole in his big toe."

"Who shot him?"

Edna looked at him pityingly. "Who the hell do you think?"

Jackson got it. Grover Buchanan was the most accident-prone person he had ever known. "Well, go nurse him back to health."

"Yeah, and if he don't behave, I'll shoot off his other foot." With that she was out the door.

Jackson went back in his office. He had two hours to kill before going over to the Largents. He swiveled his chair around to his PC and clicked on his search engine. When the screen came up, he typed in MARY DOBBS MCDERMOTT. He was rewarded with seven hundred hits. He scrolled up and down and finally selected information on her early life, thinking that it wouldn't hurt to start with a little background information.

Mary Dobbs McDermott was born in a small town in Oklahoma to Sadie Muggs and Reverend G. Hugh McDermott, a traveling evangelist. The family was poor, as her father gave away most of the small amount of cash that he received from the collection plate.

Jackson rolled his eyes. Apparantly, the daughter did not share her father's commitment to charity.

There were pictures: shots of three little girls, clad all in white, holding hymn books and singing; many of little Mary standing on a stool behind the pulpit, brandishing a bible and delivering a sermon. Her little fist was raised high and her face was contorted with emotion. He could see a part of the congregation, a sea of faces gazing at her with rapt admiration. Bet she was one spoiled brat, Jackson thought. What kid wouldn't be?

He abandoned that page and pulled up a more current item. Here was Mary Dobbs McDermott standing behind the pulpit at her church near Dallas. The lighting made a perfect halo around her head, and in her white robes she might have been a real live angel standing there. There were more pictures of various services at the luxury church, or temple, as he learned she preferred to call it. The Temple of the Holy Spirit was the name on the sign in front of the massive parking lot.

Jackson scrolled through more pictures, shots of the worship services, social events, healing services. He stopped at one picture and leaned forward. He enlarged it and examined it closely. Sure enough, standing at the altar rail, tears streaming down his face, was Tom Delgado. Sister McDermott had her hand on his head and her face to the heavens.

There was not one word about her having been a showgirl in Vegas. Not surprising. She had surely used another name for that — assuming it was true.

Jackson hit PRINT and leaned back in his chair while the printer did its work. He removed the page from the printer and, folding it carefully, put it in his coat pocket.

The phone rang and he picked it up. "Jackson Crain."

"Judge Crain." It was a woman's voice that he couldn't identify. It was breathy and almost a whisper. "This is Angie Sparks."

"I beg your pardon?"

"Angie Sparks. Remember me?"

Now he remembered. The agents meeting. She had been the chubby one who had told him about Deke and Tom arguing.

"How can I help you?" he asked.

"Oh, no. It's how I can help you." Her voice reminded him of Marilyn Monroe singing "Happy Birthday" to President

Kennedy. What was up? She hadn't sounded like this at the meeting. "I have evidence," she said, "really hard . . . evidence."

Jackson felt the hairs on the back of his neck prickle, a sure sign of danger. But, he thought, what if she did have evidence. "Excellent." He tried to make his voice sound hearty. "What is it?"

"Oh, it's too sensitive to give out on the telephone," she said. "Come over to my house and I'll . . . give it to you."

Shit! Jackson thought. "Well, I'm a little busy now. Can you give me an idea what this is about? Maybe we could meet somewhere tomorrow. Dickie's Deli?"

"No," she said. "Come on over, Jackson. I'll be waiting."

"Wait," Jackson said. "I don't know where you live."

"At 305 Hummingbird Street," she said, "in Wildewood. The little white house with the picket fence."

Jackson called the Largents to say he might be late and left the office. He drove through town to the small subdivision east of town called Wildewood. He drove around until he found Hummingbird. The house was small, but neat and well maintained. He got out and opened the gate. The side-walk split as it led up to the house, and in

140

the center stood a small fountain with a statue of a barely draped woman holding a water jug above her head. The water splashed from the jug. He went up to the pink front door and rang the bell.

When she appeared at the door, his mouth dropped open. She was holding two drinks in her hand. She was clad in a sheer black peignoir that reminded him of something out of a black-and-white 1940s movie. It left absolutely nothing to the imagination. He could see folds of white flesh through the material and huge breasts that hung down like sacks of birdseed.

"Come in," she breathed. "I've made us a little drink."

He could tell that she had already had a few. He stood on the doorstep sweating and staring. He couldn't take his eyes away from the apparition that stood before him. Her perfume wafted out the doorway to his nostrils. It was sickeningly sweet. Yet he stood there like a stone, wanting to run but unable to.

"Well, come in, silly," she said. "Haven't you ever seen a woman in a negligee before?"

"Uh, I just remembered. I've got an appointment." He finally found his voice. And turning, he sprinted back to his car, and his tires skidded on the pavement as he drove out of there.

CHAPTER NINE

Sometime between the time that Vanessa and Steve Largent had spent their evenings lying on the beach in Florida drinking wine, making love, and dreaming of the day they would own a large home and have lots of children and animals, sometime between that time and the day Steve was discharged from the Air Force, an unexpected event occurred. Steve got the call to preach the gospel.

Free-spirited Vanessa was disappointed, but she made the best of it, living in tiny, cramped parsonages furnished with other people's castoffs because she loved Steve so much. But the first dream never left her thoughts. Then a very odd thing had happened.

As quickly as it had come, Steve's call to the ministry left him.

"I still want to do God's work," he said one day. "But not as pastor of a church."

"Then how?"

"I don't know. In a way that directly benefits somebody right now, not pie in the sky after you die."

"But that's the Christian message. You told me so yourself." They were sitting in the swing out back of the tiny Baptist parsonage in Post Oak.

Steve put his arm around her. "Honey, I still believe that. It's just that I don't feel called to preach it anymore."

"Well, what then?"

"I'm praying about it, and I know the answer will come."

And it did come, in the form of Ray and Myrtice Rice. The elderly couple had been living in their large mansion since they married back in the thirties. Everyone thought they were wealthy. Ray had a reputation for being an old skinflint because he never spent a penny he didn't have to. The truth was that they were broke and barely getting along on his Social Security check. They were in real danger of losing the house.

When Vanessa and Steve found out about their situation, Steve said it just might be the answer to his prayers. Vanessa asked why, and Steve told her. They agreed that it was an excellent idea and approached the old couple about buying the house. The

Rices would, of course, be allowed to live there for the rest of their lives. Vanessa and Steve wanted to turn it into a home for unwanted children. The Rices agreed enthusiastically, and soon the big house was filled with youngsters of all ages, two very large dogs, three cats, a hamster, and two turtles.

Ashley McBride, Patty's best friend, had come to them after tragedy struck and she lost both parents. She had been a model child — until lately. Now something was worrying both Ashley and Patty, and the Largents planned to meet with Jackson Crain and try to get to the bottom of it.

Vanessa stood at the large kitchen table slicing pound cake while Steve put on the coffee. There was a brief rap on the door, and Jackson walked into the kitchen.

Vanessa took one look at him and said, "What's wrong with you, Jackson? You look like you've just been chased by a bear."

"More like a randy real estate person."

Steve turned from the coffeepot. "There's a story behind that, I can guarantee."

"Tell," Van ordered.

"Sorry. Not for publication," Jackson said. He took a deep breath. "Ham for supper?"

Van opened the oven door to give him a peek, and he found himself looking at the largest ham he had ever seen. "My God! I'd like to see the hog that thing came off of."

Steve poured three mugs of fragrant coffee. "Ham with biscuits and red-eye gravy tonight, ham sandwiches for school lunches tomorrow, ham salad on the weekend, and a big pot of bean soup cooked up with the bone for Sunday supper."

Jackson took the coffee Steve offered and found a seat at the kitchen table beside Van, who immediately passed the cake plate to him.

"What's going on with our girls?" she asked. "Ashley's personality has done a complete three-sixty."

"Patty's, too," Jackson said. "Let's compare notes, Maybe you know something I don't."

"Or vice versa," Van said.

"Doubtful," Steve said. "Ashley used to be the family chatterbox. Now she has shut down completely. She heads for her room as soon as she gets home. She won't come out until the next morning, I don't guess . . ."

". . . except that we have a rule that everyone has to show up for meals unless they are sick. And I'm the judge of that — no malingering allowed," Vanessa put in.

"But she just eats her food and asks to be

excused," Steve added.

Jackson downed the last bite of cake. "Same with Patty. She just goes in her room and turns on that stuff they call music."

"So, what do we do?" Vanessa was perplexed.

"Read their e-mails? Listen in on their phone conversations? I'm willing to try anything," Steve said.

Vanessa looked shocked. "You can't do that!"

Jackson leaned forward. "Maybe not yet . . . but don't take it off the table. They're kids, you know. And if they're in trouble, it's our job to find out and protect them."

"You're probably right, Jackson," Vanessa said. "It's just that the whole idea appalls me. Our philosophy here is all about trust. We tell the truth to the kids, and they have responded in a wonderful way. Except for very few exceptions, they don't lie to us."

"I agree, Van," Steve said. "But right now, I'm for doing whatever it takes."

"Mandy says it's their age," Jackson said.

Vanessa got up to stir something on the stove. "I don't think so," she said over her shoulder. "Not so suddenly, and not both at the same time. Girls aren't put together that way. And even with the hormones raging, they don't normally isolate themselves from their family. In fact," she smiled, "I made it a point to let the whole world know about my misery, making my family miserable in the process. That is, until my mom made sure I understood that that wouldn't be tolerated. After that I learned a little self-restraint. No, I think something else is bothering Patty and Ashley. Think hard, Jackson. Has anything happened in Patty's life that could have caused this?"

Jackson thought. "Well . . . there is one thing, but it doesn't involve Patty." He told them about his conversation with Cap Hilliard at the Texaco station.

"Well, that's something," Steve said. "We'll certainly look into that. Ashley doesn't need to be running with that bunch."

"I'll try to have a talk with her," Vanessa said. "In the meantime, Jackson, you should probably make another stab at talking to Patty. She may be in with them, too."

"Believe me, I will." Jackson drained his coffee and stood up, "Shall we just agree to keep each other posted for now?"

"Yeah," Steve said, "but I'm not waiting long. There's no telling what kind of mess they could be in, alcohol — even drugs."

Jackson frowned. He hadn't let himself

even consider that, and he didn't want to now. He moved toward the door. "Thanks for the cake, Van. It's going to spoil my supper, and Lutie Fay will be all over me."

Steve put his hand on Jackson's shoulder. "Don't worry, pal. We'll get to the bottom of this. This kind of stuff just comes with the job of raising kids. It's not the first time Van and I have had to face up to messed-up young'uns."

The next day was Friday. Jackson was sitting in his office watching the rain spattering on the flat roof of the building's portico. No storm, this. This was a steady, gray, pounding rain that farmers and gardeners liked so much. It soaked into the soil instead of running right off the way a downpour would. The phone rang and Jackson saw that Edna had picked it up.

"He's right here," he heard her say. "Jackson, it's for you."

"Judge, this is Tad Padgett. I wonder if you have time to come up to my office around one today."

"What's up?" Jackson asked.

"I want to interview the lady preacher again and, to be honest, that woman intimidates the hell out of me. I need backup."

"She's driving in from Dallas?"

"She already had an appointment to meet with Bob Kohl over at the bank. I just asked her if she'd mind talking to me about the case. She said she could spare thirty minutes."

"Gracious of her. You could have her subpoenaed."

"I know, but she is an important woman."

Jackson shook his head but agreed to the meeting. At 1:00 he was sitting in Tad's office waiting for the lady to show up. At 1:20 she came.

She was dressed in a stylish and expensive-looking raincoat with a hood. When she removed it and spread it on a chair against the wall, she revealed a severe navy blue suit and a soft white blouse with a bow at the throat. Her ash-blond hair was put up in a twist in the back, and was brushed smoothly away from her face, which Jackson noticed for the first time was pocked with acne scars. Her eyes were steely gray, like ball bearings, and seemed to look right through you, and her makeup was impeccable. She wore pearls in her ears and a gold cross around her neck.

"Forgive me, gentlemen," she said. "My business at the bank took longer than I expected. Now" — she got right down to business — "what can I tell you that I haven't already?"

"Do you mind if I record this?" Tad asked.

She nodded coolly. "I have nothing to hide. Record away."

Tad spoke the date and time into the machine, and then turned to Mary Dobbs McDermott. "Sister McDermott — is that the proper way to address you?"

"Yes."

Tad looked at the yellow pad in front of him. "Then would you just tell us in your own words how you first met Tom Delgado and what your relationship with him was?"

She half smiled. "*Relationship* is a loaded word, but yes, I'll tell you. I met Tom on a cruise to Cancún, Mexico. He was vacationing there with his wife, and I also was taking a short break from my duties."

"Were you traveling alone?"

"What an odd question. Yes, I was what you call 'alone,' although one is never alone when one is walking in the footsteps of Jesus."

Tad, who was Roman Catholic, looked embarrassed, but went on. "So you met the Delgados on a cruise?"

"Yes."

Jackson shifted in his seat. This could take all afternoon. If this woman only had thirty minutes to give, Tad had better shake it up some.

But Tad was methodical. "And how did that come about?"

"We were seated at the same table at dinner. When we found we were all from Texas, we started talking, and before long we were doing a few things together. I, of course, witnessed for the Lord as much as I could. My words fell among thorns with Dovie, but Tom, well, he was fertile soil. He couldn't get enough of Christ's message."

Couldn't get enough of you is more like it, Jackson thought.

She continued, speaking clearly and into the machine. "After we got back home, Tom expressed an interest in attending services at my temple. It was not long before he accepted Jesus Christ as his personal savior and was born again."

"And did he come every Sunday?" Tad was doubtful. It was over one hundred miles from Post Oak to Dallas.

"No, of course not. Tom found a bible-based church here that he attended. I counseled with him by phone, and he made it to our services whenever he could. He soaked up the message like a sponge. When he died, he was preparing for his sanctification ceremony. What a fine Christian man he made! One of my finest conquests."

Jackson put up his hand to cover a spontaneous grin. Conquests, indeed. Was that a slip of the tongue, or did she really call her converts "conquests"?

"What is that?" Tad asked. "Sanctification ceremony, I mean."

"It's basic to our religion. I suppose you might compare it to confirmation in the Catholic Church. A person searches his soul and makes a list of all the sins he can think of, from his entire lifetime. That takes time and much prayer and soul searching, as you might imagine. When he is ready, he stands before the congregation and gives his testimony; in other words, he confesses his sins out loud for all to hear. After that, he is baptized by the spirit and with water and is welcomed into the Body of Christ." She paused and reached for her purse. "And that about covers it. May I go now?"

Tad put up his hand. "Just one more question, please."

She frowned but leaned back in her chair. "Go ahead."

"Why did you tell us you were at a church meeting when you were actually here in Post Oak at the time of Tom Delgado's murder?"

CHAPTER TEN

Mary Dobbs McDermott was silent for a long moment. "How did you find out?"

"The judge here saw you. Tell her, Judge Crain."

"He's right," Jackson said. "You ran me off the road that day. You seemed to be in a hurry to get out of town."

The minister was unruffled. "Yes, you're right, Judge. I was in town that day. I was returning from Shreveport, and I decided to stop by and leave off some religious tracts for Tom. He wanted to put them into the folders he passes out to new prospects. His little way of witnessing, he said."

"Then why were you in such a hurry to get away?" Tad asked.

She smiled. "Get away? Young man, I was in a hurry to get back to Dallas. I had services that night." Her smile grew wider. "You thought I was running away?"

Tad turned off the recorder and stood up.

"Thank you, Sister. You have cleared things up for us. More than likely, we won't be bothering you again."

Sister McDermott paused at the door as she was leaving. "Is there any place in town where I might get a sandwich to eat on the road? I haven't had time to eat lunch."

"Try the deli on Main Street," Tad said. "It's fast — and good."

After she left, Tad looked at Jackson. "What do you think?"

"I think she's not telling all she knows, but who ever does? We know more now than we did, at least."

Tad nodded. "Well, thanks for sitting in."

Jackson left Tad's office and went directly down to the jail. The sheriff was in his office talking on the phone. "Luther, I've told you before, and I'm telling you again. We can't keep Mike Broder's cows out of your pasture if you don't keep your fences mended . . . Yeah, well, you see what you can do . . . Okay, you're welcome . . . g'bye."

Sheriff Gibbs looked at Jackson and shook his head. "Folks think they can solve all their problems by callin' the law. I'm gettin' too old for this job, Judge. Patience is all but gone."

"Got a question," Jackson said, taking a seat opposite the desk. "When you searched

Tom Delgado's office, did you find any religious tracts?"

"Them little pamphlets? Yeah, we did. Right there on the corner of Tom's desk. They're still there if nobody's moved them."

"All I wanted to know," Jackson said. He got up to go, and then sat back down. He gave the sheriff a brief rundown on the Mc-Dermott interview. When he finished, the sheriff frowned.

"It ain't good, Judge, havin' different folks working a case on their own. That young DA ought to have called me in on it."

"I agree," Jackson said. "I think he's just so green, he doesn't know the ropes."

"Well, I'd be grateful if you'd clue him in."

"I'll do that," Jackson said.

When Jackson got home, he checked the messages on his answering machine. There was one from Angie Sparks: "Jackson, I hope I didn't scare you off. I really do want to get to know you better. Won't you give me another chance? Come by for a drink tomorrow after work. I have important information about Tom's death. Please? I'll see you then — fivish?"

Jackson deleted the message. Fat chance, he thought. He doubted now that she knew anything. She only wanted to snag a man, and he was number one on her list. Jackson had had plenty of experience dodging women. After Gretchen died, single women of all ages had shown up at his door bringing pies and cakes; his married friends had tried to set him up. He had resisted them all — until Mandy came along.

After supper, Jackson decided he had had enough of Patty's moodiness. He went up to her room. "Turn down the music."

Patty looked surprised at the tone of his voice but reached over and cut off the CD player.

"I want you down in my den . . . now."

Patty got off the bed and meekly followed him downstairs. He sat down on the leather couch and pointed to a spot next to him. "Sit."

She sat. He saw that she was trembling, and a tear rolled down her cheek.

She's scared, he thought. I've never so much as raised my voice to her, and now I've scared her. He wanted to take her in his arms, but something told him it was important that he follow through on this.

"I want you to tell me what's going on with you."

"I can't, Daddy. I would if I could, but I can't."

"Why?"

"Can't you just trust me? I don't ever lie to you. I just can't."

He took her hand. "Honey, I know you don't lie. And I believe you when you say you can't — but you just think you can't. You can tell me anything. Is it about boys? I've heard that Ashley's running with a bad crowd. Are you doing that?"

"No, Daddy — and that's the truth."

"Booze? Drugs?"

"Oh, Daddy, please! Now, that's just too stupid for you to think I'd do that stuff."

And he knew it was.

"Okay, if you say so, I believe it. But so far, you've told me what it's not. Now, what *is* the problem?"

She scooted closer to him, as she had as a small child. "Daddy, it's not my secret to tell. I'm just worried, that's all. But I promise you, it's not about me. Okay?"

"About Ashley?"

She paused a minute, and then nodded her head.

He put his arms around her. "Okay, baby, but you have to promise me one thing. You'll tell me just as soon as you can."

She nodded against his chest, and he hugged her tighter, wishing that was all he needed to do to keep her from harm.

The next day was Saturday. Jackson got out of bed, showered, and dressed in jeans, a polo shirt, and his cowboy boots. He was oddly excited about the idea of going out to the Kruger ranch for lunch and a ride with Roxanne. After he dressed, he sat on the side of the bed and dialed Mandy's cell phone number. She picked up on the fourth ring.

"Hey," he said.

"Oh, hello, Jackson."

"Pretty formal greeting for someone you sleep with." He tried to keep his voice light, but the chill on the line was palpable. "How are you?"

"Fine. Jackson, I don't have time to talk now. I'll call you back." And the line went dead.

He slammed down the phone. That was it. What the hell did she take him for? The answer to that was plain. She took him for a damn nuisance who persisted in calling and bothering her. Fine. As far as he was concerned, she could stay in Victoria forever. He was going to spend the day with a captivating woman, and he intended to enjoy the hell out of it.

The spring day was perfect. Along the roadway leading to the Kruger ranch, wild plum trees showed off their dainty white blossoms. The pears were showier but just as white. As he passed Beeson's peach orchard, he was delighted to see orderly rows of neatly pruned peach trees glowing pink against the cerulean blue sky. Bluebonnets, Indian paint brush, and yellow bitterweed lay on the meadows as if someone had spread a brightly colored blanket there to dry in the sun. At eleven he drove up the cedar-lined driveway to the Kruger house. Roxanne was waiting on the porch wearing jeans, boots, and a loose-fitting white shirt. Her hair was tied in a ponytail.

"Come on," she said. "We've had a change in plans. We're not eating pattypan squash after all."

"Oh, no," Jackson grinned. "And I drove all the way out here thinking about those squash."

"No, you weren't. You were thinking about me. Admit it."

Jackson smiled but said nothing.

"Come on in. Would you like something to drink?"

"I'm fine," Jackson said as he followed her into the large den. He had not been in this room. It was lined with bookshelves holding a few books, but mostly artifacts from the family and photographs of Roxanne at every age: as a baby in an elaborate lace bassinette; at about three, riding a Shetland pony and dressed in full western regalia; away at boarding school as a young teen, dressed in soccer gear; a glamour shot of her from her college years, wearing a black drape over her shoulders. Jackson looked closer. She was clearly beautiful enough to have been a model or an actress if she had wanted that. But he was convinced that she was much more beautiful now, with some age and character lines in her face. She was not merely beautiful now; she was spectacular.

Roxanne came up behind him. "My rogue's gallery," she said.

"I think it's wonderful to see how you've changed over the years."

She shrugged. "I'll just pick up a few things and we can be off." She looked at his boots. "I see you came ready to ride. Alex and Juan have the horses saddled. We're going to have a picnic lunch."

Jackson nodded. He wasn't crazy about eating on the ground and sharing his food with insects, but women seemed to like the idea.

When she left, he strolled around the

room, looking at more of the items on the shelves. One picture showed Mrs. Kruger flanked by two ranch hands. She was holding up the head of a deer she had just shot, a twelve-point buck. Jackson didn't hunt, but he knew that that was a big deal in the hunting world. More shots showed Roxanne as a child, ranch hands gathered around a cook fire, the family on a large ship. Roxanne as a teenager had that bored look that the young affect when they are forced to associate with adults. He didn't notice that she had walked up behind him.

"Wasn't I a little twit? My parents made me go with them to Germany. I didn't want to leave my friends at home."

Jackson turned and smiled at her. "Nice to know you were just a regular kid."

"What's that supposed to mean?"

"Well . . . you're anything but 'regular' now, you're . . . amazing." What the hell was he doing?

He almost thought she leaned into him, but before the thought could form, she was moving across the room. "We'd better get a move on. The boys have the horses waiting for us." She picked up her sketch pad and pencil bag off the hall table and carried them under her arm.

Jackson walked beside her around the

house, through a rail fence to the large barn out back. Alex stood holding the reins of two horses, a large bay and a palomino.

"The bay's yours," she said, patting the palomino on the neck. "This is Potato Chip. He's mine. He's old, but there's still a lot of spirit left in him. Right, Chips?" She nuzzled the horse's neck, and he turned his head toward her. "Oh, and your horse's name is Satan," she said with an evil grin.

Jackson took Satan's reins and patted the horse's neck. "We'll get along just fine, won't we, buddy?" he whispered in the animal's ear.

They walked the horses down a lane that led toward an expanse of open land. When they reached the edge of the grassland, she nudged Potato Chip's flanks, and he broke into a run. Satan didn't need much urging to follow suit. Clusters of cows looked up curiously as they galloped by, and then went back to grazing in the lush, green coastal Bermuda meadow. Jackson noticed that she was leading him toward a tree line. Probably a creek up there, he thought. But she stopped beside a small outbuilding and dismounted before they got halfway there.

"Mind if I sketch this building?" she asked. She was already withdrawing her pad and pencil bag from her saddlebags.

"Can I watch?"

She was walking around examining the building, noticing how the light fell on it from the various sides and angles. "I don't care." She was suddenly preoccupied. "Have to work fast before the light changes." She drew a small, collapsible easel from her saddlebag and quickly set it up facing the building.

"What is this building for, anyway?" Jackson asked.

"Used to be a bunkhouse for hands back in the old days. Now we just use it to store hay and feed."

Jackson watched as she worked. She sketched fast but with sure and confident strokes. As if by magic, the dilapidated old building appeared on the page. Jackson thought of the magic picture book someone had given him as a child. You simply rubbed the lead of a pencil on the page and a picture magically appeared. She was that quick. She flipped over the page and moved the easel to a different angle. Finally, he found a shade tree and dropped down on the soft pine needle–covered ground under it. He watched, more interested in her than her work, until she closed the pad and returned it to the saddlebag.

"Come on, lazybones," she called. "We'll

be late for lunch."

Jackson mounted Satan. "Where is all this taking place?"

"It's a surprise." She pointed to the distant grove of trees. "Those trees are a good mile away, but it's worth the ride. I promise."

She turned Potato Chip's head toward the trees, and they rode in comfortable silence the rest of the way, she seemingly pre-occupied with scanning the countryside for sketching sites, and he just enjoying East Texas in the spring. As far as Jackson Crain was concerned, there was no better place in the world.

As they neared the tree line, Jackson spotted a deer fence, a seven-foot-tall chain-link barrier designed to keep deer from jumping over it. "You have a deer problem?"

"Not too much," she said over her shoulder. "It's mainly for coyotes. They're not such a bother singly, but in a pack, they can take down a half-grown calf." She led him to a clearing in the pines, where he was surprised to see a large blue cooler waiting for them.

"Cookie brought this out earlier," she explained.

They tethered the horses beside a nearby stream, and Roxanne opened the cooler. A

Navajo rug was folded neatly on the top. Jackson took it and spread it on the ground, while Roxanne began laying out the food. She took out plastic plates and flatware, paper napkins. Finally, a gallon of sweet iced tea with mint leaves floating inside.

"For a city girl, you know a lot about ranching." Jackson bit into an egg salad sandwich.

"Wasn't always a city girl." She reached for more tea. "Remember, I grew up on this ranch. My daddy took me with him from the day I could mount a horse." She grinned evilly. "I could castrate a bull by the time I was twelve."

Jackson cocked an eyebrow. "That should make interesting dinner chat for your city friends."

She laughed. "Great little conversation starter. You'd be surprised how many beaus I've picked up with that one."

For some reason Jackson didn't like to think about that, so he lay back on the pine needles and looked up at the sky through the tree branches. Before he knew it, he had fallen asleep. When he opened his eyes again, she was sitting beside him, sketching him.

"Dirty trick," he muttered.

"Don't move. I'm almost through." She

drew a few more lines, and then turned the pad around toward him.

"Damn," he breathed. It wasn't exactly like him, but she had captured the essence of a contented man, relaxed and happy, sleeping off a big meal.

"If you want it, it's yours," she said. "But I'll keep it here until we get back to the house." She folded the pad and again placed it in her saddlebag. "Get up, lazy, I've got something else to show you. We can walk there."

He followed her down a cattle trail through the trees until they came to a deep trench, eight feet wide and extending as far as the eye could see from north to south. As he looked down its length, he could see honeysuckle vines growing on either side. Jackson climbed down and stood in the middle, looking both ways. She followed and stood beside him.

"Is it . . . ?"

"Yes, the Cherokee Trace. The Indians planted the honeysuckle and these." She plucked a small pink blossom off a thorny shrub Jackson had not noticed. "Know what this is?"

"A Cherokee rose," he said. He had heard all his life that the Trace ran through Kemp County, had heard of the Cherokee roses, but this was the first time he had actually seen it, and he had a feeling of awe. He could almost hear the pounding of moccasined feet, the barking of dogs, the clip-clop of ponies, and the occasional wail of a baby as they traversed this trail of tears on their way to the Oklahoma Territory. "It's almost like church, isn't it?"

"Oh, much better," she said. "I used to come here and just lie for hours. It was like they were talking to me through the wind in the trees.

He took her hand and they stood listening to the wind sloughing through the pine needles above, not talking until finally, they did hear voices in the wind. She turned to him, and he kissed her, a long and sweet kiss with no hint of passion, only the knowledge that they had shared something profound and not to be forgotten here among the pines.

CHAPTER ELEVEN

Jackson was jerked back to reality the minute he reached home. Lutie Fay didn't usually come in on Saturdays, but she stood in the kitchen today stirring a big pot of peach preserves. Sterilized jars stood upside down on a clean dish towel on the kitchen table.

"You better call the sheriff," she said. "He been callin' since noon. He say you call him the minute you get home."

Jackson went into the den and called the sheriff's office.

"Judge, you barely caught me," Sheriff Gibbs said. "I was just about to go out to the scene again."

"What's happened?" Jackson wanted to know.

"That preacher lady was found in her car out at that rest stop three miles from town. She was shot through the head."

"I'll ride with you," Jackson said.

"When did they find her?" Jackson asked as the sheriff turned the car out of the jail parking lot.

"Early this morning. A trucker found her and called it in. We got her over at the hospital morgue. Car's been towed in. It's settin' right back of the jail. So far, nobody's shown up to claim the body." He took a deep breath. " 'Course that young DA'll be a damn fool if he don't order an autopsy."

"Weapon?"

"Well, that's dicey. She had a gun. It was in the glove compartment. Hadn't been fired. No prints except hers. Looks like the killer brought his own gun. There was a bullet hole in the windshield right where her head would have been. That says she must have seen who shot her. Fat lot of good that does. She ain't gonna tell us."

They drove through town, past the high school, and turned onto Farm Road 9, which would take them to the Dallas highway. Jackson looked out the window, wondering what was going on here. He was damned sure this murder was related to the Delgado killing. Was it possible that Dossie really did do it? She sure had no use for

Mary Dobbs McDermott.

The sheriff pulled the car into the lane that led to the rest stop. Several trucks and a black Subaru Outback were parked well away from the taped-off crime scene. The occupants of the Outback, a family, were having a picnic at one of the concrete tables provided by the state of Texas.

"Should've cordoned off the whole damn place," the sheriff grumbled.

Dooley Burns was sitting at a table near the scene.

"Anybody been messin' around?" the sheriff asked.

"Had to run some kids off," Dooley drawled. " 'Bout all."

Jackson and the sheriff walked around the scene checking the asphalt parking area for anything that might have been overlooked in the initial investigation. Jackson picked up a purple toothpick. "She must have stopped at the deli," he said.

"What's that?" The sheriff's head came up.

"The DA and I interviewed her just before she left town. She asked about a place to get a sandwich for the road."

"Well, I'd be mighty interested in knowing how that went. Hell, Judge, am I the sheriff around here, or not?"

"DA's got a tape. Besides, I filled you in."

The sheriff nodded and prodded the ground with his toe. He picked up an empty shell casing and held it up for Jackson to see.

"And . . . ?" Jackson said.

"Could be important," the sheriff said. "This here's a .22 rifle shell. Her gun was an automatic." He put it in his pocket. The two men walked back to the table where Dooley was still sitting. Jackson stepped up on the bench and sat directly on the table. The sheriff sat on the bench below.

Just then a red BMW drove up and Tad Padgett got out and walked toward them. "Thought I'd find y'all out here," he said. "Finding anything?"

The others shook their heads.

"What about inside the car?"

"Clean as a whistle," the sheriff said. "Her gun was in the glove compartment. Her briefcase was in the backseat. Oh, and there was a sack from the deli on the floor. Nothin' but a few potato chips inside. I got all that at the office."

Tad nodded. "Anything on the next of kin?"

"She's got two grown children, a son and a daughter. Both in Kansas somewhere. They didn't have nothing to do with their mama. Estranged, doncha know. Some people from her church are supposed to be gettin' here tonight to claim the body."

"That won't be possible," Tad said. "I've ordered an autopsy. Doc will do it tonight. We'll get the gross results right away. The lab work will take a week or more."

Jackson nodded. "Good deal."

"Ditto on that," Tad said. He turned to Jackson. "Think it's related to the Delgado murder?"

Jackson just looked at him.

"Sorry. Of course it is. And now it's looking even worse for Mrs. Delgado."

"Have you questioned her?" Jackson looked from the sheriff to Tad. They both shook their heads.

"Judge," the sheriff said, looking at his watch. "I've got time to talk to her right now. How about going with me?"

"Let's go," Jackson said. He looked at Tad. "You coming?"

"You think I should?"

"No," Jackson said. "Three men knocking on her door might scare her. The sheriff here will tape it for you."

Dooley was lying flat out on a bench with his hat over his face. The sheriff nudged him with his toe. "Stay here, Dool, and try to stay awake. I'll come get you directly."

Dooley nodded and managed to arrange himself into a sitting position.

It was close to six when they drove up to the Delgado house. The sun was going down and the tree-shaded yard was nearly dark. They walked up the front steps to find Dovie sitting on the veranda with a drink in her hand.

"Hidy, Mrs. Delgado," the sheriff said, putting one foot on the first step. "Can we come up and talk to you?"

"Of course." Dovie sipped her drink. "Hello, Judge Crain. Can I offer you something?"

"No, thanks. I'm afraid we've got some upsetting news, Mrs. Delgado. Mary Dobbs McDermott was found shot in her car this morning."

"Dead?"

"Yes, she was dead."

"Well." Dovie put her drink down. "What do you know about that?" She looked at Jackson. "But, I don't know why you think that would be upsetting to me. I hardly knew the woman who stole my inheritance. Why should I be upset?" She threw back her head and laughed. "As a matter of fact, I find that I'm not upset in the least. Instead, I'm rather pleased. The bitch is dead. *Hi-ho, the bitch is dead,*" she sang, and

Jackson knew then that she was very drunk.

He motioned to the sheriff and they left, explaining that they would talk to her the next day.

"Which old bitch, the witchy old bitch . . ."

It was eight o'clock when Jackson got back home. As soon as he entered through the back door, he heard the television playing in the den. He pushed open the door and found Patty curled up on the couch. She jumped up and ran to him, throwing her arms around his waist.

"Oh, Daddy. I'm glad you're home."

"Me, too. What did I do to deserve a hug?"

She went back to the couch and sat down. He joined her. "Well?"

"I've been a jerk lately. I just want you to know that I'm, like, over it."

"Mind telling me what it is you're over?"

"Everything. I just decided I can't take on another person's problems."

"That's very mature of you — but, honey, if Ashley's in trouble, maybe her guardians ought to know."

"Daddy, it's her secret, not mine. So, let's you and me hang together tonight."

Jackson pulled away and looked at her. He didn't know what had brought about this change. Had the situation improved, or was it just that at her age, she couldn't maintain such a high state of emotion for long? Whatever the reason, he was grateful.

"Sure you want to spend the evening with your old dad?"

"Yep."

"Then I've got an idea. Why don't I go in and make some popcorn, and you pick out a movie to watch."

"Awesome." Patty got off the couch and went to the cabinet where they stored their motley DVD collection. She held one up. "How about *Groundhog Day*?"

Jackson was already heading for the kitchen. "Good one."

He looked in the pantry and found a packet of popcorn. He shoved it in the microwave, waited while it popped, and then poured it into a bowl. He grabbed two sodas from the fridge before returning to the den. Placing the drinks and bowl on the coffee table, he took a seat at the end of the couch. Tonight, he decided to forgo his club chair to be closer to his child. She stretched out on the couch and put her head in his lap, and they sat for two pleasant hours just being together.

When the movie was over, Jackson removed the DVD and cut off the television. He came back to the couch and looked at

Patty, who was rubbing her eyes and stretching.

"Bed for me," she said. "And no school tomorrow. Yea!"

"Honey, if you do need to talk about Ashley's problem, whatever it is, you know you can trust me. Right?"

"Right," she said. "Night, Dad."

CHAPTER TWELVE

The next day was Sunday. Jackson awoke to the sound of rain drumming on the roof outside his bedroom. He looked out the window at the street below. The sound of the wind in the elm trees combined with the peppering of the rain felt cozy and good. He was reminded of rainy days in this house when he was a small boy. Florine would make light, fluffy pancakes for his breakfast, and he would spend the day playing with his toys on the rug in the den, feeling safe and protected listening to the low voices of his mother and Florine talking together as they went about their work. It felt good when he caught the scent of steak or fish frying in the kitchen and greens bubbling on the stove. Back in those days, *lunch* had been *dinner,* and it had been the main meal of the day. His father would come home precisely at noon, dressed in his black suit, white shirt, and black string tie. Sometimes he would invite other lawyers or business friends to eat with the family, and the good china and crystal glasses would be brought out.

Jackson got dressed. He had made up his mind to whip up a batch of Florine's pancakes, eat them with warm maple syrup and butter, and settle down in his den with the Sunday paper. Beyond that he had no other plans except to move around as little as possible.

When his pancakes were ready, he sat down at the table and ate six, washing them down with coffee. After he finished, he rinsed his dishes and put them in the dishwasher. He headed for the front porch to bring in the newspaper and stood for a moment at the door looking at the rain falling on the street he had grown up on. It hadn't changed much in all those years. The lawns were still wide and green, and the houses, mostly built in the teens and twenties, were well kept with neat flower beds and well-trimmed sidewalks. Satisfied with what he saw, he picked up the paper and went back into the house.

He sank down in his club chair with a sigh and, after lighting a Don Diego cigar, began to read. After an hour, he folded the paper and took it to the trash can on the back porch. He looked at his watch. It was only 10:30. He still had a whole day ahead of him. He decided to go upstairs and check his e-mail. Not much on Sunday, he thought, but it was something to do.

He turned on his computer and waited for it to boot up. When the desktop came on, he clicked MAIL and found he had only two. One was from a political organization. He deleted that. The next came from an address he was unfamiliar with. He opened it and read:

Jackson,
It pains me more than you'll ever know to write this. You have meant so very much to me, but something has happened here in Victoria. I have fallen in love all over again with my old sweetheart, Hector. We were together in high school, but because of my foolish pride, we broke up. Now we have met again and Hector's love for me and mine for him is still as strong as ever. I must be with him. Jackson, I hope you will understand and that you will tell Patty that I love her and will never forget her.

Affectionately,
Mandy

He quickly printed the e-mail and read it again. So that was why she had been so strange on the telephone. She was seeing this other guy and feeling guilty about it. Well, old Hector could have her. Jackson had thought they'd had something special together, but apparently he was wrong. He sat down on the edge of the bed. There was a time when he'd thought that life without Mandy would be unbearable. But now he felt nothing. She had been gone for such a long time, and her recent attitude when he called her had been cold and had hurt him. It was true; he felt nothing.

He went down the hall and tapped on Patty's door. "Pats, you up?"

"Kinda," came a muffled voice.

"I left you some pancakes on the table. Want me to heat them up for you?"

Patty stuck her head out the door. "Hey, Daddy. I'm having a granola bar. You can eat the pancakes."

He patted his midsection. "I'm full. I'll just chuck them. You coming down?"

"Uh-huh. Minute."

Jackson went back downstairs and poured himself a third cup of coffee. He sat at the table to wait for Patty. She had to be told about Mandy, and he wanted to get it over with. She would be hurt, maybe more than he was. But she had to know. He sat and watched as she drank a glass of milk and downed a granola bar.

"Daddy, you're creeping me out. Why are you watching me like that?"

Jackson took the folded piece of paper out of his shirt pocket and shoved it across the table to her. "I don't know any better way to tell you, honey. Read that."

She unfolded the paper and read it. Her face set in a frown. "She sent you an e-mail breakup? That's like the lowest thing a person can do. What a coward. She couldn't call you and tell you in person?"

"I thought you'd be all broken up about it. You and Mandy were pretty close."

"*Were* is right," she said. "We're not close any longer." She looked at him. "Daddy, you're the best man in the world, and any woman ought to know that. She's just stupid, that's all. And as far as I'm concerned, she doesn't exist!"

Jackson got up and came around the table. He put his arm around her shoulder and gave her a hug. He was too moved to speak. His little girl was growing up.

"So, what would you like to do today?" he asked. "I'm all yours."

She grinned at him. "Well, Daddy, you're just going to have to entertain yourself today. I'm going over to Sara Taylor's house to study for a civics test. Her mother said that if you'll drive me over, her daddy will bring me home after supper. Okay?"

"Sure, honey. When are you going?"

"Soon as I get dressed. We're going to watch a movie before we start studying."

When he got back from the Taylors' house, Jackson was at loose ends. Mandy's e-mail had managed to ruin his perfect lazy Sunday. He went into his den and turned on the television. Might as well watch a little golf. Jackson wished it was football season. He could forget his troubles watching a good football game. Golf only made the afternoon drag slower. He turned the set off and picked up the phone. He looked at it. He didn't even know why he had picked it up. Who was he going to call? Without thinking, he dialed the Kruger number. Roxanne answered.

"Hello, there, Jackson Crain. Want to take me out to dinner?"

Jackson couldn't help smiling. She was the most direct woman he had ever met.

"As a matter of fact, I was thinking about that. Thing is, this is Post Oak. There's no place to go."

"Ah, but there is. Cookie told me that Dickie over at the deli is trying something

183

new. He is turning his place into a bistro at night. Wine . . . candles on the tables . . . French country food."

"I'll pick you up at seven," Jackson said. "We really should help Dickie make a success of this."

"Of course," she said, with that husky laugh of hers.

The rain had stopped around two, leaving the trees heavy with moisture and the air fresh and clean. It was dark when Jackson drove once again up the cedar-lined driveway and, as before, she was standing on the porch waiting for him. She was wearing black slacks with a white silk blouse. Her hair was held back severely with a large black bow at the neck. Gold chains hung around her neck. She looked so, well, so *New York* that he was almost intimidated by her. She had seemed to fit so perfectly with her surroundings in their earlier encounters. Now she was a stranger.

She must have read his expression, because she grinned. "Too dressy for night life in Post Oak?"

"Who cares?" he said, relaxing. "You look just like the woman I want to be seen with."

A few cars were parked in front of the deli when they arrived. Jackson was relieved. He had had no idea how the townspeople would react to a bistro in their midst. He should have known better. Dickie would have plenty of business until everybody had satisfied their curiosity. After that, he would have to prove himself with excellent food.

Dickie met them at the door wearing a tuxedo. "Judge Crain! I'm so glad you came." He led them to a table next to a window and held Roxanne's chair as she seated herself.

Jackson looked around the room. Dickie had spruced up the place for the dinner hour. Small arrangements of purple flowers surrounded tall green candles on each table. The green-checkered cloths he had seen before had been replaced with starched white. The napkins were large and also white.

"What do you think?" Dickie asked. "Will Post Oak take to a place like this?"

Jackson looked around the room. The place was almost full. "Sure," he said. "As soon as you take that toothpick from behind your ear."

Dickie grinned sheepishly and removed the toothpick. He took their wine order, and then left after handing them large menus.

"He's really gone all out." Jackson was amused.

Roxanne fingered the delicate purple

violets on the table. "I think it's charming."

Jackson left it for Roxanne to order for the both of them, since he had no idea what most of the menu items were. They each had flaky little pies filled with scallops and shrimp bathed in a creamy wine sauce, salads, and for dessert, crêpes suzette, which Dickie prepared at the table with elaborate flourishes.

As they talked, Jackson's eye fell on a couple across the room. It was Deke Slade and Brenda Barns. They were leaning across the table toward each other and talking intensely.

"Do you know those people?" Roxanne asked.

"Not well. They both worked for Tom Delgado. She was with Dickie when they found the body. Why do you ask?"

"The man came out to the house to try and list the ranch. There was something a little snaky about him, so I sent him packing."

"Not very tactful of him to come so soon after your mother's death."

She shrugged. "A good salesman strikes while the iron is hot. Look, they're coming this way."

Sure enough, Brenda and Deke were weaving through the tables toward them.

Towering over the table, Deke leaned toward Roxanne. "Miss Kruger — and Judge Crain." He paused as if the conversational ball was in their court.

Roxanne nodded coolly. "Mr. Spade, is it?"

"Slade." He looked irritated.

"Of course," Roxanne said. "Forgive me."

He colored and turned toward Brenda. "This is Ms. Brenda Barns, another associate from our office. Have you made a decision about selling the ranch?"

Jackson noted that Brenda ever so slightly eased away from him, disassociating herself from Deke's heavy-handed methods.

Roxanne chose to ignore him and simply sipped her wine.

Jackson decided to step in. "Miss Kruger is a client of mine," he said. "We haven't made any decision about selling the ranch."

He turned back to his dinner, and after an awkward minute, the couple eased away from the table.

"What a jerk," Jackson said.

"He can't spoil my fun," Roxanne said, spearing a tiny mushroom with her fork and waving it at him. "I'm here with a handsome man, and I plan on making the best of it."

Dinner took over an hour, and Jackson

found himself relaxing as he had not done in a long time. Roxanne told him funny stories about her life in the city and, when he told a yarn or two about Post Oak, she laughed delightedly. When they left, he didn't want the evening to be over.

"Would you like a drive before I take you home?"

She looked at him under her lashes. "What I would really like is for you to come home with me and sit beside me on the porch swing to listen to the tree frogs and katydids. It's been my favorite evening sport since I came home."

"Hey," Jackson said with a laugh, "whatever floats your boat. But first, I'll have to call my daughter. She's studying at a friend's house."

Helen Taylor answered the phone. "Jackson, they're still hard at work. Would it be possible for Patty to stay all night? I'll bring her home early in the morning so she'll have plenty of time to get dressed for school."

For once, Jackson didn't care whether it was a school night or not. He definitely did not want this evening to end.

"Well, if you're sure it's no trouble," he said. "I guess that would be okay."

He hung up the phone and grinned at Roxanne. "I'm all yours," he said, opening the car door for her.

They didn't talk much as they sat on the swing. The squeaking of the chains mingled with the night sounds all around them. It was unusually warm for March, and a gentle breeze ruffled her hair as they rocked back and forth.

Later, Jackson didn't know why he did it, but he found himself telling her about Mandy. Later, he thought what a bore he must have been talking about an old girlfriend to this beautiful and fascinating woman. She listened without speaking.

"I don't know why I told you all that," he apologized.

She stood up.

Well, now you've done it, chump, he thought.

She took his hand. "Come inside with me. I think I've got just what you need."

He followed her inside, and it didn't take long to discover that she was absolutely right.

CHAPTER THIRTEEN

Mae Applewhite came bustling into the Knitters' Nook. She was wearing a turquoise patio dress with bright pink ruffles around the sleeves and hem and flip-flops.

"Don't anybody say a word about how I look," she said. "I was just finishing the christening dress I'm making for my niece's baby, and I ran out of thread. It's that white baby yarn."

Esther leaned across the counter while Jane went to fetch the yarn. "Coffee?"

"I believe I will," Mae said, sinking down into the rocker that always stayed next to the show window. "I'm pooped already, and it's not even nine o'clock yet. I don't know what's the matter with me. Doctor says I may need to take iron shots."

Esther came out carrying a mug of coffee. She held it away playfully as Mae reached her hand out to take it. "Tell me something I don't know," she said.

"Okay. Annie Mae and Vernon Oakley's oldest daughter, Meghan, had been accepted into veterinary school at A and M this fall. Annie Mae says it's a big deal. She says it's harder to get into vet school than real medical school."

"Well, sure." Jane was putting Mae's yarn into a pink paper bag. "Vets have to learn all about turtles, hamsters, pigs, birds . . . and I don't know what all. People doctors only have to know about people."

"Um-hum," Mae said. "This is real good coffee, Esther. I also heard that Angie Sparks has set her cap for Jackson Crain."

"She'll have to get in line," Jane said. "He's already got Mandy, and now I hear he's been beating a path out to the Kruger ranch."

"Who's Angie Sparks?" Esther wanted to know.

"She's an agent in Tom Delgado's office. Plump? Big hair? I know you've seen her, Esther. She goes to our church."

"Anyway, if I may, she was in the fellowship hall after church talking to anybody who would listen about how he came over and had a drink with her the other night. And the way she told it, he stayed on past the cocktail hour, if you get my meaning."

"Well, if that's true, he's got two women

on the string," Jane said. "Tell her, Esther."

"Oh, this is good," Esther said. "Well, Jane and I worked late last night getting our quarterly reports out. I declare, the government's going to put all us small-business people right out on the street with all their paperwork."

"Get to the point," Jane said.

"Well, we were walking home past the deli. Dickie's serving dinner now. Did you know that?"

Mae shook her head.

"Anyway, we peeked in, and guess who we saw eating there?"

"Everybody in town?"

Esther giggled. "Just about. But who we saw was Jackson and that Roxanne Kruger. And that's not all. They were looking mighty lovey-dovey, if you ask me."

"Well," Mae said. "I never! I didn't think he had it in him. Two women, indeed!"

Just then, the bell on the door tinkled, and Annabeth Jones came in. "Am I missing anything?"

The other three filled her in.

"Well," Annabeth wondered, "what do you suppose Mandy's going to think about all that?"

"Nothing," Jane said. "She's dumped him."

The others looked at her in shock. "No!" they said in chorus.

"Yep. Nan Glass came in yesterday. You were gone out, Esther, and I forgot to tell you. Nan said her granddaughter came home from school saying that Patty told her Mandy had dumped her daddy for some old boyfriend down in South Texas. Good riddance, if you ask me. Jackson didn't have any business marrying a Mexican."

"No, Jane, that's not nice," Esther said.

Mae changed the subject. "There was quite a crowd down at the courthouse when I passed just now. What do you suppose is going on?"

"I'll find out," Jane said, picking up a stack of stamped envelopes. "I need to go to the post office anyway."

When Jackson pulled into his reserved parking place in back of the courthouse the next morning, he was greeted by a chaotic scene. Mobile units from the Dallas television stations, their telescoping towers reaching as far as nine feet into the air, were parked in the lot. They represented the four major national networks. He saw marked cars from the Tyler and Longview stations, smaller venues, but just as eager to cover the story. A crowd of curious locals had gathered to take in the excitement. Jackson looked toward the jail and saw a miserable Sheriff Gibbs trying hard to field the barrage of shouted questions from the reporters. He looked helplessly at Jackson.

Jackson paused a minute, and then pushed his way through the crowd to stand beside the sheriff. He leaned over and whispered something into his ear. The sheriff nodded and held up both his hands.

"Ladies and gentlemen! Hey, I'm tryin' to tell you something here. If you don't shut up, you ain't going to hear it!" The reporters continued to shout questions at him. Finally, the sheriff had had enough. "Shut up, goddamnit!"

They quieted down immediately.

"This here's County Judge Jackson Crain. He's got something to say to you."

Jackson took one of the microphones a reporter handed him. "There will be a press conference at eleven on the courthouse steps. At that time, we will try to answer your questions as well as we can without compromising our case. Now, please disperse until then, and give us a chance to get our work done. Thank you."

With that the sheriff went back inside, and Jackson followed him.

"Thanks, Judge." Sheriff Gibbs sank

gratefully down in his squeaky desk chair. "You sure saved my bacon."

"It was bound to happen," Jackson said. He looked out the window. "When these guys get out of the way, I'm going up to talk to Tad. He needs to be at that press conference."

"Reckon you better," the sheriff said. "That little peckerwood sure does like to get noticed."

"He has political ambitions." Jackson stood up and headed for the door.

When he got back outside he saw that the crowd of reporters had gotten back into their vans or ambled down the street in search of refreshments. Jackson walked briskly across the parking lot to his office. Edna was sitting at her chair with a big smile on her face.

"Holy shit! That was some show. Did you see me looking out the window at the end of the hall?"

"Nope," Jackson said. "I told them we'd have a regular press conference at eleven. I'd better go up and let Tad in on it."

"Reckon you had," she said. "That boy's going to want to be right in the big middle. He wants to be governor some day. Did you know that?"

"Heard something," Jackson said. He sat

195

down at his desk and dialed Tad's number. He quickly filled the DA in on what was going on.

"Well, damn," Tad said. "I never heard a thing."

"Thought I'd come up and fill you in," Jackson said.

"Come on. I've got something I want to run by you, too."

When Jackson was seated in the DA's office, they went over the evidence in the case and decided what they could share with the press. There was not much.

"I guess I'll just go out there and do what those fellows do on TV," Tad said. "Just tell them the basics and no more."

Jackson nodded.

"You want to be there?"

"Nope. I'm not officially on this case. You and the sheriff should handle it."

"Okay." Tad drew a file off the corner of the desk. "I've got to do something that you're not going to like, Jackson. But the circumstantial case against Mrs. Delgado is growing every day. I'm going to have to bring her in."

"What charges?"

"Capital murder."

Jackson shook his head. That meant no bond. It looked like the sheriff and Norma

Jean, his wife, would have to deal with having Dossie in their jail.

"What's happened?" he asked.

"We got the ballistics back on the gun that shot the preacher lady. It's the same one that shot old Tom."

Jackson was dumbfounded. "You mean the gun Dossie buried? How can that be? You've got that gun in the evidence cabinet."

"Well, their faces are red over at the lab in Tyler. It seems that Dossie's gun didn't match after all. When they got the slug out of Sister McDermott, it matched the one they dug out of Tom. And neither one came from the buried gun."

"And that implicates Dossie? Seems to me like it would be just the opposite."

Tad's boyish face took on a self-satisfied smirk. "That's what you might think. It's not the way I look at it. The way I look at it is, she's the only one with the motive to kill both of them. And, I might add, the opportunity. Her maid says she disappeared on Friday afternoon for four hours and wouldn't say a word about where she'd been." He leaned forward and placed his hands flat on his desk. "You show me one other person who had a motive to kill them both, and I'll let her out with a big bouquet of red roses and an apology."

"And you've questioned her about those four hours?"

"Sure. She says she was depressed and felt like a drive in the country. Said she went out to the lake and just sat on a bench watching the water. Didn't see a soul the whole time."

"Well, that does look bad," Jackson admitted. "But she could be telling the truth. After all, she has been through a shock. Maybe she just wanted to go off by herself for a while."

"And maybe she was off killing Mary Dobbs McDermott," Tad said emphatically. "I can't take any chances, Judge."

"So, when are you going to bring her in?"

"Just as soon as I can get rid of these media people. Gee, Jackson, if I can crack this case, I'll be known all over the state."

Jackson nodded. *And if you screw it up, you'll still be known all over the state,* he thought.

When Jackson got back to his office, he put in a call to Curtis Gilmer. "They're going to arrest Dossie," he said.

"I heard," Curtis said. "Tad just called and told me. Nice of him, I guess, but Jackson, you know I'm no trial lawyer. I called her daddy, and he's retained old 'Bulldog'

Hicks from Houston. He'll be here by the time they turn the key on her cell door."

Reginald "Bulldog" Hicks was the most famous trial lawyer in Texas. If he couldn't get Dossie off, nobody could. And, on top of that, he could show Tad Padgett a thing or two about attracting publicity.

As soon as Jackson hung up, Edna stuck her head in the door. "Horace Kinkaid's here to see you."

Jackson nodded.

Horace came in with a pad and pen in his hand. He sat down in one of the clients chairs in front of the desk.

"Have a seat, why don't you," Jackson said.

"Yessir, think I will."

"What can I do for you?"

"Well, it's this way," Horace said. "They got that press conference going on downstairs. It's a regular Chinese fire drill. I says to myself, I says, Horace, how come you want to be down here gettin' stepped on by these city fellers when you can just go on up and see your old friend, Jackson, and get the story out of him?"

"That's what you said, huh?"

"Yep. So give, old buddy."

"Sure," Jackson said. "I'll tell you everything they're telling that crowd down there."

"Fair enough," Horace said. "And, Jackson, maybe you could just throw in a fact or two that they ain't going to get. For old friendship's sake, doncha know."

"Ask away." Jackson put his feet on the desk and reared back with his hands behind his head.

"Any connection between the lady preacher's murder and Tom Delgado?"

"We're looking into that," Jackson said.

"Got any evidence to support that idea?"

"Can't say. Ongoing investigation." Jackson was beginning to enjoy this.

"Well, do you have any suspects?"

"There have been no arrests made at this time."

"Hell and damnation, Jackson. You sound like the White House press secretary. Ain't you going to give me anything?"

"It's not my case," Jackson said. "Talk to the DA about it."

"Okay, is it true that Tom left all his money to that McDermott woman?"

"That's public record. You can look it up."

"Okay, here's one last question. It's lunchtime. How 'bout we sneak out the back door and go get some grub?"

"Deal," Jackson said. "But no more talk about the case."

"Hey, Jackson," Horace said, as they got

into Jackson's car. "I'm fed up with that sissy food old Dickie puts out. How 'bout a big old greasy burger at the Dairy Star?"

"Great idea!" Jackson agreed completely. He was hungry for red meat, and the Dairy Star put a full half-pound patty on their burgers, plus a slab of real cheddar cheese, none of that imitation stuff.

When they walked into the place, it was more crowded than usual. Students were allowed to leave campus for lunch, and this was their favorite hangout. Jackson and Horace stood at the door and scanned the place looking for a table. It was then that Jackson saw Ashley sitting in a booth with Marvin Tidwell. She was crying while he talked to her urgently. Jackson quickly turned away before she spotted him.

"Let's just go through the drive-through and eat in the car," he suggested.

Horace nodded, and they went back to the car. After they got their burgers, Jackson found a spot under a tree, and they sat eating and drinking silently. The burger was just as good as Jackson had imagined.

Horace popped a crispy fry in his mouth. "Hey, Jackson, wasn't that poor old Joe Junior McBride's girl in there?"

"Yep."

"Well, what the hell is she doing with that

201

Tidwell kid? Everybody knows that boy's bad news, just like his old man."

"Well, now, I just don't know," Jackson said, irritated.

Horace forged ahead. "You might not know this, either. Marvin Tidwell and his gang busted out all the windows down at the Ford place. I'm talking about those big showroom windows."

"You've got to be kidding. I would have heard about that."

"You might have, if old Biff Covington had've brought charges. Thing is, he didn't. Hushed the thing up as fast as he could and made out like it was an accident of some kind."

"Why the hell would he do that?"

"He would do that on account of Mutt Tidwell is one hell of a badass. As you prob'ly know, old Biff ain't the smartest banana in the bunch. Well, Mutt told him if he went to the law, something bad might just happen to his wife and little girl. That sealed it. Biff's plumb crazy about that little girl of his. His wife's another matter. That is one mean woman — ugly, too. Biff might of gone to the law on it just to get rid of her — but not the kid. Nosiree, Bob."

Jackson finished the last of his hamburger and wadded up the paper it came in. "So, how did you find out about it?"

Horace patted his nose with his index finger. "Nose for news, pal, nose for news."

Jackson didn't say anymore. This was looking bad for Ashley. He'd have to have another talk with the Largents.

After dropping Horace off at the news-paper office, Jackson went back to the courthouse. His calendar was clear, so he picked up the phone and dialed the Lar-gents' number. No one answered. He left a brief message stating only that he needed to talk with them and would stop by on the way home from work.

On an impulse, he dialed the Kruger ranch. Cookie answered the phone and told him that Roxanne had left early to go sketching.

"She gets up every morning, and soon's she's had her breakfast, she saddles up Potato Chip and heads on out with her art supplies. Judge, that little woman sure is crazy about drawin' and paintin'."

"Well, thanks, Cookie. Will you tell her I called?"

"Sure will, Judge."

Jackson hung up the phone and sat look-ing out the window. He couldn't get Ashley off his mind. She had looked so helpless, sobbing there in that booth. At four he told

Edna that he was going home for the day.

She nodded. "Might as well, you've got a shitload of work on tap for tomorrow. Commissioners Court, remember?"

Jackson groaned. He hated Commissioners Court day. It was an endless meeting to discuss the workings of the county. The commissioners always jockeyed for more money or equipment for their precinct, and Jackson had to preside.

"See you," he said, and went out the door.

When he came in the back door, he heard Patty's voice. "Daddy, is that you?"

She came bounding down the back stairs and ran to him. She threw her arms around him, sobbing.

"What is it, honey?"

"It's Ashley. She's going to get an abortion! Oh, Daddy, you've got to stop her."

He looked down at her. "What do you know? Where are they going? And when?"

"They're leaving at five. And I don't know where they're going. Someplace out in the country, I think."

"Think, honey. Did she say anything that would give you a hint?"

"There's a nurse over there that does abortions in her house. That's all I know. Oh, Daddy, I tried to talk to her, but she was like she didn't even know me. She just walked away — wouldn't say a word."

Jackson had a pretty good idea where they were going. Polson's Mill was a small community in the county east of Post Oak. It was known as a place law-abiding people avoided at all costs. It was a rough place. It had always been a hangout for bootleggers and thieves, but lately there had been rumors of meth labs as well.

"Could it have been Polson's Mill?" he asked Patty.

She nodded vigorously. "That's it. I remember now. Hurry up, Daddy. You've got to stop her."

Jackson went to the phone and dialed the Largent house. "Meet me at the jail right now," he said when Steve answered. "It's about Ashley."

"Daddy, what are you going to do?"

"Stop them." He was already halfway out the door.

CHAPTER FOURTEEN

Jackson and Steve arrived at the jail at the same moment. Without speaking, they went to the door and rang the bell. When the sheriff opened it, Jackson explained the situation to both men at the same time.

"Birdie Pew," the sheriff said. "I know her. Oh, yeah." He grabbed his hat. "Follow me. I'll radio Peters on the way. He's their constable, doncha know."

Steve got into the car with Jackson, and they left the parking lot behind the sheriff's car. The road to Polson's Mill wound through dense forests and low creek bottoms. Its curves were dangerous and not well marked. Wrecks on that road were a regular occurrence. Jackson knew the route well, but even so he was having trouble keeping up with the sheriff, who was wasting no time.

They rode into the village, which was nothing more than a wood frame post office and a shabby convenience store with one gas pump out front. Following the sheriff as he turned down an unpaved road, they saw small houses and mobile homes and children playing in the murky water that filled the ditches along the road. The sheriff pulled up in front of a wooden house with flaking yellow paint. A red pickup was already parked in the driveway, so they stopped on the road in front of the house. Ashley and Marvin Tidwell stood on the front porch, apparently waiting for someone to come to the door. Marvin held a tight grip on Ashley's elbow, and they could see a red welt on the side of her face.

"Ashley!" Steve Largent called.

Ashley turned a tear-stained face toward him. With a sudden move, she wrenched her arm free from Marvin and ran toward him. "Brother Steve!" She buried her face in his chest and sobbed as he spoke softly to her and stroked her hair. She looked up at him, and there was no doubt that she had been struck — hard. Her lip was red and swollen, and her face was already turning black-and-blue. A crescent-shaped mark ran from her eyebrow to her cheekbone.

Steve Largent's face grew grim.

"What did he do to you?"

She looked at the ground. "He hit me with

a flashlight. It hurt, Brother Steve."

At that, Jackson remembered how young she was, only fourteen, just a child.

Sheriff Gibbs walked over and took Marvin Tidwell by the arm. He walked him off the porch and handcuffed him. "How old are you, kid?"

"Nineteen next month." The boy stuck out his chin and glared at the sheriff.

"Excellent!" The sheriff grinned. "You can be charged as an adult. What do you think, Judge? Aggravated assault? Assault on a minor? Statutory rape?"

"Those'll do for starters," Jackson said.

Sheriff Gibbs walked the boy to his car and put him in the backseat.

Just then the door opened, and a very large blonde stuck her head out.

"What's goin' on out here?"

"Afraid you've just lost a patient, Birdie," the sheriff said. "We're taking these two kids home."

"Don't know what you're talkin' about, sheriff," she said around a wad of gum the size of a walnut. "I don't have patients."

"Better keep it that way," the sheriff said. "On account of, if I ever catch you doing your dirty work on one of my Post Oak kids . . ." His face grew red, and Birdie backed away from him.

"Well, I don't guess you need me right now — do you?"

"Git on in the house," the sheriff growled.

A car drove up and the Polson's Mill constable, Rex Peters, got out. "Everything under control?"

The sheriff eyed Ashley and Steve and motioned to the others to step away from them. "For now it is. We rescued this young girl from Birdie. That's good. But, naturally, we didn't catch Birdie in the act. That would have been bad, but it would have been evidence." He glanced nervously at the man and the girl. They were now walking toward Jackson's car. Steve opened the door and got in back with Ashley. "Well, you know what I mean," the sheriff continued. "Thing is, I want that woman. Peters, I want you to watch her — drive by here day and night. We'll get her yet."

Peters nodded. "You got it, sheriff. That old woman is about as rotten as an old bucket of fish heads."

Back in town, Jackson dropped Steve and Ashley at their house and drove home. Patty met him at the back door, concern written all over her face.

He put his arm around her. "We got there in time," he said. "She's home now, and Marvin's in jail."

Patty nodded. "Why's he in jail?"

"Oh, legal stuff you wouldn't understand. But, I will tell you this. He hit her." She would know soon enough. Might as well come from him.

"Can I call her?"

"Better not tonight. She's still pretty upset. Why don't you wait 'til tomorrow?"

"Okay. Well, I've got homework. Lutie says your supper's on top of the microwave."

She went up the back stairs and Jackson went into the kitchen to see what Lutie had left. The phone rang, and he picked it up.

"I heard you called."

He took a deep breath. "I did. Cookie said you were working."

"Well, I was, but that's not why I called. I want you to come to dinner tomorrow night."

He didn't hesitate. "Okay."

"Come at seven. I don't cook, but Cookie is making us a nice casserole and a salad. Bring wine."

"I'll be there."

"You sound tired."

"Tell you about it tomorrow."

He hung up the phone and, whistling, went to inspect his supper.

The next morning they arrested Dossie

Delgado.

Jackson waited until the Commissioners Court meeting broke for lunch and went down to see her. What he saw made his eyes open wide. Her cell looked like a hospital room. Flowers were lined along the walls and, on the small washstand, he saw a bowl of fruit and a box of chocolates. Dossie was lying on her bunk with a monogrammed towel draped over her eyes.

"Don't that just beat all?" the sheriff said. "Her friends are coming around here every few minutes bringing her stuff. You'd think she was sick, not incarcerated."

They walked away from the cell. "How is she?"

"Ain't said a word to me since me and Dooley brought her in. I heard her talking to Mae Applewhite, though."

"What are the charges?"

"Murder one. That's just for Tom. Tad says he's gonna try her for the preacher lady separately."

Jackson looked grim. That young DA needed a dose of reality.

"Any word from her lawyer?"

"He'll be here this afternoon I hear. That's what Curtis Gilmer says. Says she's got that Bulldog Hicks feller from Houston. He's the big gun, Judge."

"That's what I hear," Jackson said. "Well, I'll be back later. I want to talk to her when she's able."

Commissioners Court ended at three, and when Jackson got back to his office, a man he had never seen but recognized from his pictures in newspapers and television sat waiting for him. Jackson was surprised to see that he was a small man, not over five feet five, wearing an expensive pin-striped suit and highly polished eel-skin cowboy boots. He held a Stetson hat in his lap. His face was pockmarked, and his hair was either white or very blond. It was hard to judge his age. He could be forty or seventy. He looked at Jackson with intelligent blue eyes and got to his feet.

"Reginald Hicks," he said extending his hand. "They call me Bulldog."

Jackson smiled. "I know. Come on in." He led Hicks into his office and offered him a chair. "Can I get you anything? Coffee? Soft drink?"

The man shook his head. "I hear you're familiar with the Dossie Delgado case — and I hear that you thought it was a big mistake to arrest her."

Jackson nodded. "I don't think she did it."

"That's what I wanted to hear. Can I

count on you for help?"

"Depends on what it is."

Hicks grinned. "Smart man. Don't let the city guy slicker you."

"What did you have in mind?" Jackson asked.

Hicks opened his briefcase and drew out some papers. He spread them on Jackson's desk. "Here's the complaint. Take a look at it and tell me if you see anything wrong."

Jackson picked up the papers and read them. They were signed by District Judge C. Oliver Jones. "Can't see that I do," he said. "Charged with capital murder on the evidence that she had means and motive. Looks to me like he had enough to charge her — convincing a grand jury is another matter."

"Look at this right here, and here, and here." Bulldog pointed with one stubby finger.

Jackson saw what he meant. The complaint was a sloppy piece of work. The defendant's name was spelled wrong, the date was wrong, and whoever typed it had put in "Kant" County instead of Kent County. "Mess," Jackson acknowledged. "But what good is it? A few typos can be corrected in ten minutes."

"Um-hmm," the other lawyer said. "But it

just might buy us a little time. I reckon I could get her out of jail on the basis of this."

"For a few hours," Jackson said. "I don't see what you're getting at."

"There's more than one way to skin a cat. Now, were there any more suspects?"

"Not in Tad Padgett's mind. He focused in on Dossie from the git-go."

Bulldog shifted in his chair and crossed his legs. "Planning on making a name for himself."

"That's about it," Jackson concurred.

"More suspects? Who found the body?"

Jackson had a feeling Bulldog Hicks had already found that out, but he answered, "The local caterer and one of Tom's agents. I take it you read the crime report."

"Got me there," Hicks said. "Anybody question those two?"

"Matter of fact, I did," Jackson said. "Not much there. I don't know whether law enforcement checked their stories or not."

Bulldog stood up. "Can I count on your help?"

Jackson stood also, towering over the little man. "I'll do what I can."

The other lawyer took a card out of his breast pocket and handed it to Jackson. "My cell phone number is on there. I'll be staying at the Post Oak Inn, room twelve."

After the man left, Jackson sat for a long time at his desk. An hour later he had a plan of sorts. At least, he thought, there are a few things I can do. He got up and went into the outer office. Edna was taking a break and drinking a diet soda.

"I'm out of here," he said.

She raised the drink can like a toast. "Enjoy your evening."

"Oh, I plan to," he grinned at her as he headed for the door.

"Jackson! Jackson, don't you dare leave like that. You're keeping something from me, aren't you? Jackson!"

But he had already closed the door quietly behind him.

CHAPTER FIFTEEN

When Jackson got home, Patty was sitting at the kitchen table shelling peas for Lutie Fay, who was checking a hen she had baking in the oven. He planted a kiss on Patty's head and went over to where Lutie was standing.

"I'm in trouble," he said.

"How come?"

"I'm going out for dinner, and I forgot to tell you."

Lutie glared at him. "Well, ain't that just ducky. What am I supposed to do with this nice dinner I'm makin' for you?"

He put his arm around her and kissed her cheek. She shrugged away from him but couldn't hide a smile. "You ain't gonna sweet-talk your way out of this."

Just then, the phone rang. Patty made a dive for it. "Yes, ma'am, he's right here." She extended the phone to Jackson.

Vanessa Largent was on the other end.

"Jackson, I wonder if you might be willing to let us have Patty for the night."

"It's a school night," he said, confused. Most parents in Post Oak had a standing rule: no overnights on school nights.

"I know," she said. "But Ashley needs cheering up, and the only person she wants to see is Patty. Besides, Jackson, I've got three other kids to get off to school. One more won't be a stretch. And I'll make sure she does her homework, too. It would be a real favor, Jackson. Ashley's not ready to go back herself just yet. In fact, I may home-school her for the rest of the semester. But she really needs her friend right now."

"Well, if you put it that way. Here's Patty. I'll let her decide."

Patty took the phone. "Yes, ma'am! I'll be ready. Okay, yeah. Homework? I don't have any. Okay. 'Bye."

She turned to Jackson. "She's picking me up in ten minutes. Gotta go pack." She started out of the room, and then turned back and threw her arms around Lutie's waist. "I'm sorry, Lutie."

Lutie gave her a little squeeze and patted her on the rump. "Run on and have a good time," she said.

Jackson went upstairs, showered, and changed into casual slacks and a knit shirt.

He looked at his watch. It was only 5:30. He had time for a Scotch and a cigar before leaving the house. But when he got downstairs to the den, he sat down at the computer. He found a search engine and typed in the name of Deke Slade. There was something about that guy that didn't compute. He had the look of a hood — granted he was dressed up in expensive clothes, but a hood just the same. And he stood out like a sore thumb in little Post Oak. Slade had said he'd had known Tom before coming here, and now he knew he was telling the truth. When the result came up on the screen, he saw what that connection was. Tom Delgado's construction company popped up, and there it was: Deke Slade had been his building superintendent. Might be something there, for sure.

Now he typed in Tom Delgado's name. A surprising number of hits came up. It seemed that Tom had not always been in the construction business. He had also dabbled in banking, electronics, and, only recently, vinyl siding, and then real estate. Jackson stared at the screen. Vinyl siding? Somehow, that didn't fit. He clicked on that link and saw that before he married Dossie, Tom had owned a siding company. He and Deke would come into a medium-sized city and saturate the area with advertising. After doing slipshod work on all the jobs they could get, they would move on to another town. Jackson noted that several complaints had been placed with the Better Business Bureau and the states' attorneys general offices in his name.

Apparently, Tom had become respectable only after he married Dossie. He searched further and came upon another business. Tom Delgado and a partner had owned a start-up long-distance telephone service. Jackson checked the date: late eighties to early nineties. About that time the phone companies had been deregulated. Jackson recalled that a number of new phone companies had come into being, the majority of which had gone under. He read the name: Extel. Certainly, he had never heard of that one; not surprising, it had its offices in San Francisco.

Jackson searched Extel. Again, he got a number of hits. Extel had lasted less than two years, and in the end, Tom Delgado and his partner were indicted for running a pyramid scheme. The company recruited "partners," who went out and sold the service, but more important, they recruited other "partners," who recruited others, on down the line. Soon an area was saturated, leaving subscribers complaining loudly about the shoddy service, but by then the original partners would have moved on to greener pastures.

Jackson scrolled on down and found a newspaper account of the case. Tom and his partner stood in front of the courthouse. Jackson looked closely at the picture. He didn't need to look further. He knew who the murderer was.

Jackson stopped by the liquor store on the way and picked up a good bottle of red wine and a good bottle of white wine. On impulse, he added a bottle of champagne to his purchases. He felt festive. Just being with the fascinating Roxanne Kruger was cause for celebration. He whistled as he stashed his purchases in the backseat of his car.

She was waiting for him on the front porch when he arrived. To his surprise, she put her arms around him and kissed him square on the lips. Then she threw back her head and laughed heartily, showing the tiny gap between her two front teeth.

"I always was a funny kisser," he said.

She laughed harder. When she could speak, she said, "I always laugh when I'm happy. And truth is, I'm happy to see you."

Jackson's heart leapt. Was he falling in love with this woman? Sure felt like it. He put his arm around her waist and led her back inside. A table had been set up in the library. A small fire licked at the grate.

Later, Jackson couldn't say what they had eaten, only that it had tasted delicious. The wine was delicious, and Roxanne Kruger was the most delectable of all.

He stayed the night.

The next morning Jackson arrived at work late and found another press conference under way. This time the star of the show was Bulldog Hicks. He stood on a box in front of a bank of microphones making a speech. Jackson went and stood beside Sheriff Gibbs and Norma Jean, who were leaning against the side of the building.

"I have climbed the Mountain of Truth," he shouted, "and what have I found? I have found lies and treachery. They have incarcerated an innocent woman, a woman who would never harm a hair on the head of one of God's humblest creatures. Would she do harm to the man she loved more than life itself? I say to you: No!" He paused for effect, leaning forward on the podium and scanning the crowd. "And now, friends, she languishes in a filthy, rat-infested jail cell . . ."

Before the sheriff could stop her, Norma

Jean had run up to stand in front of the man. "It is not!" she shouted. "You take that back. My jail is as clean as your house!" She stomped her foot.

Bulldog was unfazed. "I was speaking metaphorically, ma'am."

"Well, all right, then." Norma Jean wasn't sure what that long word meant, but his voice had sounded appeasing, so she gave him the benefit of the doubt.

Jackson glanced up at Tad's window and saw him looking out, a frown on his face. Jackson smiled to himself. That was one young lawyer who was finding himself in over his head. He turned, went into his office, and poured himself a mug of coffee.

"You look like the cat that ate the canary," Edna commented. Jackson looked away to hide a smile, but Edna was too fast for him. "What have you been up to?"

"I don't know what you're talking about." Jackson hurried into his own office and shut the door. He sat at his desk sipping coffee and reliving the night before. His pleasant thoughts were interrupted by a loud voice in the outer office. The door opened and Edna stuck her head in.

"Mr. Bulldog Hicks is here."

Without waiting for an invitation, Bulldog brushed past her and flopped down in the clients chair. "Got time for a little sleuthing?" he asked.

Jackson looked at Edna, who nodded her head. "You've got nothing until three," she said.

"What's on your mind?"

Bulldog crossed one short leg over the other. "Just wondering who else I could contact that might help Miz Delgado's case. Any ideas? Who was with her the night he died?"

"That would be Mae Applewhite," Jackson said. "A neighbor. She was sitting with Dossie when I left that night."

"You know her well?"

"Everybody knows everybody in Post Oak."

"Mind calling her and setting up a little chat?"

Jackson pulled the phone toward him and dialed. "Miss Mae? This is Jackson Crain. Are you busy right now? Setting out tomato plants? When might you be through?" Jackson listened. "Well, ma'am, Dossie's lawyer was hoping to have a little chat with you." He held the phone away from his head as the woman screamed into his ear.

"The famous lawyer from Houston? The one I saw on Court TV?"

"That's the one."

"Give me twenty minutes to make myself presentable, and then you gentlemen come right on over. I've got some sugar cookies still warm from the oven."

Jackson hung up the phone and looked at Bulldog. "You heard?"

The other man nodded.

When they rang Mae's doorbell, she greeted them wearing a fresh denim skirt with a crisp white blouse. She led them into the parlor, where they could see tea things set out on the coffee table. Jackson thought she had gone from planting tomatoes to gracious entertaining in record time.

"Dear lady," Bulldog gushed. "Why this sumptuous spread for two humble lawyers?"

Mae actually tittered. Jackson was amused.

"Why, Mr. Hicks, you're a star. Everybody in the county knows who you are — and here you are in my little house."

When they were seated around the tea table, Bulldog got right to the point.

"We're only here for one thing," he said. "And that is to help save an innocent woman from a grave miscarriage of justice."

Mae nodded.

"Do you agree with us that Mrs. Dossie Wynn Delgado is being falsely accused?"

"Oh, yes. Why, Dossie wouldn't hurt a

mouse — and she was scared to death of them."

"Then you wouldn't mind answering a few questions for us?" Bulldog reached for a sugar cookie and popped it in his mouth. "Manna from heaven," he said.

Mae tittered again.

Bulldog opened his briefcase and drew out a yellow legal pad. "Now then, Miss Mae . . . you don't mind me calling you that?"

She shook her head vigorously.

"Alright then. I suppose Mrs. Delgado must have been very broken up that night about her husband's death."

"You would have thought so." Mae sipped her tea and looked over the rim of the cup at Bulldog. Jackson could see she was enjoying herself.

"Are you saying that she was not?"

"Well . . . I wouldn't want to say that. People respond to death in different ways. Some holler their heads off and cry and all. Others take it more . . ." She looked at Jackson. "What's the word I want?"

"Stoically," Jackson said.

"Yes. That's the work. She was stoical about it. Just sat there and drank her bourbon and talked on like her husband wasn't lying dead right out there in his little office."

"What did she talk about?" Bulldog wanted to know.

"Mostly about Tom, you know. But not like he was dead. She was talking just like he was still alive and would come walking across the yard any minute."

"Can you be more specific?"

"Let me see. Well, she talked about when they first met. It was in Dallas. He was selling vinyl siding at the time. She said her daddy like to have had a conniption fit when he heard about it, but she didn't care. She said it was love at first sight for her. He was a handsome man, doncha know. And she said he rushed her off her feet. Presents, flowers, candy, the whole courtship thing. More tea?" The men shook their heads and she went on. "Dossie wasn't the best-looking woman, even when she was young. Dumpy. Didn't seem to know how to take care of herself. But she said Tom didn't care about that. She said he told her he loved the person inside, whatever that meant."

"Um-hum," Bulldog said. "What did she have to say about their lives here in Post Oak?"

"Let me think. Oh, yes. She talked about Mary Dobbs McDermott. Didn't have much use for her, I'll tell you that. She said Tom had gone and got religion and that he wasn't any fun anymore. All he wanted to do was read his bible and run up and down the road between here and Dallas and that church of hers. She said he told her he had to purge his soul. He was going to get up in front of the whole congregation and tell all the sins he ever committed. A full confession, he told her. Well, Dossie said, if he humiliated her by telling about all the women he'd messed around with since they'd been married, she take a gun and shoot him dead. Remember, she was still talking like he was still alive. It was creepy, as the kids say."

"Anything else?"

"No." Mae brushed the crumbs off her lap. "By that time, she was pretty drunk, so I just helped her up to bed. I sat with her all night long, in case she woke up and needed anything. She didn't, though. Slept like a log until eight o'clock, when the maid came. After that, I went home."

Bulldog stood up. "Thanks you, dear lady. I'm forever indebted to you."

Mae stood at the front door as the two men left. Suddenly, Bulldog turned and went back up to her. He took her hand in both of his. "Miss Mae, I wonder whether you've talked to the sheriff or Mr. Tad Padgett about what you've just told us."

Mae shook her head. "Mr. Bulldog, I watch Court TV all the time. I know about these things."

The two exchanged a look, and Bulldog squeezed her hand as he turned and left. "Thank you again for such a lovely visit."

They went down the sidewalk to their car, leaving Mae blushing with pleasure.

CHAPTER SIXTEEN

After that, the case went cold. Bulldog went back to Houston to prepare his defense, while Dossie languished in jail. Spring turned into summer. In May, Dossie developed a serious cough and, at her doctor's recommendation, Bulldog was able to convince Tad Padgett and the district judge to place her under house arrest while wearing an ankle bracelet. Norma Jean Gibbs was much relieved, and commented to her husband that she finally felt at home in her own apartment again.

Down at the Knitters' Nook, Mae Applewhite was worried.

"I declare, I don't know what's going to happen to poor Dossie." She gave the rocking chair a push that almost toppled her over.

"Why? What's the matter now? She's out of jail, at least." Jane was inventorying a shipment of needlepoint patterns that had just come in.

Annabeth Jones stopped poring over a book of crochet patterns. "Can we do anything? I just feel for Dossie so much. That district attorney ought to have somebody turn him over their knee. The idea, thinking that Dossie could have done murder!"

"I don't think anybody can do anything," Mae said. "The poor thing seems to have taken to the bottle."

"No!" Esther breathed. "And her a Baptist, too."

"A backsliding Baptist, if you ask me," Jane said. "A Christmas and Easter Baptist, is what she was. Never going to get to heaven that way."

"You're right about that," Annabeth agreed. "We went calling on her one night — before Tom died — and she just came right out and told us she had better things to do than to go to church and sit with a bunch of hypocrites. Of course, she had had a drink or two that night, I think." She rolled her eyes. "So we all forgave her, just like Jesus tells us to do."

"I declare," Mae said. "If we don't get some rain, all my tomato plants are just going to fall over dead."

■ ■ ■ ■

Life at the courthouse settled into its usual summer doldrums. Deeds were recorded, divorces filed, wills were probated automatically. The old building seemed to run on cruise control. The heat and humidity of the Texas summer made it just too much trouble to commit a crime. And all court cases that could be were put off until the weather turned cooler. The courtroom was not air-conditioned. The sheriff found himself playing dominoes at the fire station every afternoon. He played with the fire chief, the night watchman, and anybody else who happened to come along.

Jackson was confused about his feelings for Roxanne. It felt a lot like love but, being the analytical man that he was, he just couldn't accept that he could fall out of love with Mandy and in love with Roxanne in one short week.

"You think too much," Lutie said one morning, when he confided in her. "The good Lord don't give you blessings on your timetable. You take it when you can get it."

"Then what should I do?" he asked.

"Do? How come you're askin' me what to

do? I never laid eyes on the woman." She shoved a pan of cookies in the oven. "I do know this much. That Mandy done you wrong, and you got every right to find you somebody else."

"You're right," he said. "I'm going for it — whatever *it* is."

Ashley McBride was wearing maternity clothes now, and Patty was over at the Largents' house all the time. Now that things were out in the open, she was excited about the new baby. Ashley had asked her to be her Lamaze coach, and Jackson had agreed to let her do it. He had had his doubts at first, but Vanessa had convinced him that it would be a great learning experience for her.

"How many young girls have an opportunity like this?" she asked one morning over coffee. "Think how far ahead of her friends she'll be when she's ready to have a baby of her own."

Jackson sincerely hoped that that event was far in the future, but he relented and let her do it.

As for himself, he was spending all his spare time at the Kruger ranch. Some days they went on picnics or just explored the place on horseback. Other times they had dinner on the wide veranda and listened to the night songs of the frogs in the ponds. Sometimes, he just watched fascinated as she worked. She was turning her sketches into paintings. The bright tubes of acrylic colors on her canvas were transformed into the East Texas landscape. The rolling hills dotted with the trees he knew so well, persimmon, red oak, and pine, sycamore and cedar, under her skilled hands appeared in their true colors and shapes. Red and white Hereford cattle dotted the green fields. One of his favorites showed a lone buck staring out of the canvas while its white-tailed mate darted away into the cool, deep woods.

"Will New Yorkers buy these?"

"I never think about that," she replied, reloading her brush.

"I love you."

She put down her brush and turned to face him. "Don't," she said.

"Sorry," he said. "I'm down for the count."

It was in late June that the Delgado case broke wide open.

It started one Saturday morning when Jackson came downstairs to the kitchen to find Lutie sitting at the table having a cup of coffee with her cousin Fayrene, who worked for Dossie Delgado. Jackson took his favorite mug from the cabinet, filled it from the coffeepot, and joined them. He half listened as they chatted on about people he didn't know. The coffee was good and the kitchen was cool and bright. He was content to just sit and listen to their mellow Southern voices recounting the latest bits of gossip from St. Paul's CME Church.

Finally, Fayrene turned to him. "How you been, Judge?"

"Doing well, Fayrene. And you?"

"I do pretty well. I can't say the same for Miss Dossie, though. Judge, I been real worried about her."

"How so?"

Fayrene curled her three middle fingers, extended her little finger and thumb and made a drinking motion with her hand.

"Drinking a lot?"

"Yessir, you might say that."

"Well, would you say that?"

"Oh, yeah. And she's taken to letting me go home soon's I get the house cleaned up and her laundry done. She don't let me cook for her anymore. That's got me worried, too. She don't weigh hardly nothin.' " She squirmed in her chair. "Judge, I hope

I'm not speakin' up when I shouldn't, but somebody's got to do something about that lady. She just lay up in that bed with a bottle of Jack Daniel's on her nightstand, eatin' whatever somebody happens to bring by — or not. It don't matter to her."

"So, her friends are bringing food in?"

"That, and she'll order from the deli now and then, if she ain't eaten in a while. Only reason I know that is, I see the sacks layin' around the house."

"I'll see if I can get in touch with her sister in Dallas," Jackson said. "She was at the funeral. Remember?"

Fayrene nodded. "I remember. I'd sure be much obliged if you would do that, Judge. Have you got her number?"

Jackson shook his head. "Think you can get it for me?"

"Yes, sir. And I'll call you with it on Monday when I get to work. Law me, I hate to go over to that house worse than anything. Judge, I was in Mr. Tom's office runnin' the vacuum — getting it all cleaned up for the meeting. He was sitting at his desk working, just like he always did. And, bless your heart, that wasn't more than a half hour before that old murderer just walked in and shot him dead!"

Jackson nodded sympathetically.

As it turned out, Fayrene never got to work on Monday, or any other day after that.

CHAPTER SEVENTEEN

After breakfast, Jackson drove to his office and placed a call to Bulldog Hicks. When the other lawyer answered, Jackson filled him in on what was going on with his client.

"I'll get in touch with her family," Hicks said. "Anything else I ought to know about?"

Jackson assured him that there was nothing, and they ended the call.

He dialed Mae Applewhite's number.

"We do the best we can, Judge," she said. "But Dossie won't see anybody, and believe me, we've all tried. We take turns leaving a little something for her to eat every day, but most days, the plates are still out on the front porch where we left them. She doesn't even bother to take them in. Mostly we're just tired of trying. If a person doesn't want help . . ."

"I understand," Jackson said. "Well, her

sister is being called. Maybe she can do something."

"Praise Jesus," Mae said. "Now, why didn't I think of that?"

Roxanne invited Patty to come out to the ranch with Jackson to go horseback riding. When Jackson got home from the office, Patty was waiting for him. She was dressed in jeans and had put her unruly brown hair up in pigtails. She looked exactly the way she had looked when she was eight and life was so much simpler.

Three horses were saddled and tethered near the house when they arrived at the ranch. Roxanne was waiting on the porch.

"This is Patty," Jackson said, proud to introduce his daughter to the woman he now knew he loved completely.

Roxanne shook her hand and greeted her gravely. "Do you know how to ride?" she asked.

"Oh, yes," Patty assured her. "I took riding two years in a row at camp. I can even ride an English saddle."

Roxanne smiled. "I'm impressed. Don't know whether I could do that. But it won't be necessary today. We have western saddles. That horn can come in mighty handy sometimes."

They walked toward the horses.

"Which one's mine?" Patty was trying hard to hide her excitement, but it sparkled in her eyes.

"The bay," Roxanne said. "Happy's a fine old lady, and easy in her stride."

Patty went over and patted the horse's nose. Happy nuzzled her hand looking for treats. Patty turned to Roxanne, who smiled and handed her a sugar cube she'd pulled from her pocket.

As they mounted and turned the horses toward the woods, Roxanne explained, "Cookie has made a picnic lunch for us. I thought we'd eat at the Cherokee Trace. Patty, do you know about that?"

Patty wasn't paying much attention. She was busy kneeing Happy to make her go faster, but Happy was in no hurry. The three horses walked side by side until they reached open land. Then they trotted across the pasture and down the dry creek bed to the Trace. It was a perfect day for riding. The breeze was just enough, and the world around them was bright green under a bowl of cool blue.

The magic had not left the Trace. Standing in the indentation made so many years ago, with the trees making a canopy above, they could still imagine the sounds of the ghostly parade marching toward a land they had never seen.

"Awesome," Patty breathed.

"In the truest sense of that word," Jackson pronounced.

Patty rolled her eyes at him. Roxanne grinned. Jackson could be just a little pompous at times. Patty would have called it "geeky."

They tied the horses and gave them water before spreading out the picnic. Ham sandwiches had never tasted so good, washed down by sweet tea and topped off by flakey fried peach pies. After they ate, they spread blankets on the soft pine needles and lay looking up at the sky through the branches. Hawks swooped in the sky or perched in the tops of trees watching for small prey, while the huge black buzzards made graceful circles high above.

Before they left the Trace, Roxanne got out her sketch pad and made a quick sketch of Patty leaning against a tree. She signed it with a flourish and handed it over for the other two to see. Jackson saw in it the eight-year-old he remembered, the gawky teen of today, and the promise of the beautiful woman she was to become. He shook his head in wonder at this woman's talent.

Patty stared openmouthed. "Do I look

like that?"

"Exactly," Roxanne said, taking the pad back. "I'll keep this in my saddlebag, but I promise to give it to you before you go home."

They rode back to the house and ate homemade ice cream on the front porch. Afterward, Roxanne took Patty up to her studio and showed off her paintings.

When it was time to leave, Roxanne tore off the sketch and handed it to Patty. "Have this framed in acid-free paper, and it will last forever," she said. "Who knows? Some day it might be valuable."

Jackson was not fooled. He knew what prices her paintings commanded. He would see that this prize was properly cared for.

As he was getting into the car, Roxanne approached him. "Coming back later?"

He grinned. "Try and stop me. Nine o'clock?"

She nodded and waved them away.

As it turned out, he didn't return that night. Just as he was getting into his car, the loud fire siren blared all over town, summoning the volunteer firemen. At the same moment, his cell phone rang.

"Judge," Sheriff Gibbs said breathlessly, "it's the Delgado house."

Jackson drove to the center of town and saw a red glow in the sky in the direction of Poplar Street. The fire was out of control. The house would be lost. He pulled over to let the fire engine pass, and then followed it, parking a block away from the house. He sprinted toward the sheriff's car, which was parked across the street. All they could do was watch as the firemen sprayed the house. It was obviously a total loss.

"Dossie?" Jackson looked at the sheriff.

"We don't know yet. Most likely, she's still in there."

They stood and watched for hours it seemed like, feeling the heat and seeing flames spewing skyward, listening to the sickening sound of walls collapsing. The air was rancid with the acrid smoke that burned their throats and lungs. Their eyes stung from it. Still they watched in fascination. The once stately home at last was only a pile of foul-smelling charred wood, still glowing in spots where live coals lay. Small puffs of smoke shot skyward from time to time. But it was over. The firemen turned off their hoses and, weary and soot smudged, trudged back to their engine.

"Nothin' more we can do tonight," the sheriff said. "I've notified the state fire marshals to come in and investigate as soon as it cools off some."

Jackson went back home and called Roxanne to explain what had happened. After hanging up, he undressed and showered. He put on shorts and a T-shirt and took his clothes to the back porch and piled them on top of the washing machine. He went into his den and poured himself a generous Scotch and sat in his chair, where he lit a Don Diego cigar.

If this fire was arson, as he suspected, and if Dossie Delgado was dead, which he also suspected, that would mean three murders in a period of only four months — and all related. This had to stop. He thought about the information he had uncovered online, the person out of Tom Delgado's past. Now was the time to act. If his theory was right there had to be evidence to link this suspect to the murders. He finished his Scotch and went to his computer. Following the same trail as before, he pulled up the grainy newspaper photo of Tom Delgado and the suspect. He stared at it closely. No doubt about it, it was the same person, older now, but the same. He printed the image and turned off the computer. He took the copy up to his room, where he placed it on his dresser under his keys. Tomorrow, he would take it to the sheriff. At last he went to bed, the smell of smoke still lingering in his nostrils.

The next morning was Sunday. A rain in the night had broken the drought, but now the sun shone brightly again. After making breakfast for himself and Patty, Jackson read the Sunday paper with his second cup of coffee. Patty came into the room and flopped down on the leather couch.

He looked at her over his paper. "Bored?"

"Uh-huh. Sundays are boring. Don't you think so?"

"Not so much. I kind of like staying home with nothing to do. But what can I say, I'm old. Right?"

She grinned. "Right, Daddy. But I'm young, and I'm bored!"

"Why don't you practice your clarinet?"

"Boring . . ."

"Well, isn't there anything on TV?"

"On Sunday morning? Daddy, get real."

"What's Ashley doing today?"

"Don't know." She brightened a little. "Maybe I'll call." She ran out of the room to the hall phone. When she came back, she was smiling. "They're going out to the peach orchard to buy peaches, and then Ashley's going to help Van put up preserves. They said I could come along."

He cocked an eyebrow at her. "I didn't know you were interested in the preservation of fruit."

"Oh, Daddy. It's something. And anyway, I like going over there. Stuff's always happening over there."

"Unlike over here."

"Right. Will you drive me over?"

"Yep."

Jackson drove to the jail after dropping Patty off at the Largents. He went to the back door and rang the bell. Norma Jean Gibbs let him in.

"Lenny's in the office," she said. "Wasn't that awful about the Delgado house?"

"Sure was." Jackson went to the sheriff's office and tapped on the door.

"Come in," the sheriff barked.

Jackson found the sheriff sitting at his desk talking to a stranger. The man was wearing a khaki uniform with a marshall's badge on the pocket. Dooley Burns was sitting in the corner dozing in a chair.

"Have a seat, Judge. This is Officer Reedy of the Fire Marshalls."

Jackson shook the man's hand. "Find anything?"

"We were able to send a man in with a heat suit," Reedy said. "Found the woman's body — what was left of it. Looks like the fire started in her bedroom. We can't do a complete investigation until the thing cools down." He paused. "That little rain we had last night helped."

Jackson nodded. "So, there's no way to tell whether it was arson?"

"Not at this time," Reedy said. "However, our guys will probably be able to get in by tomorrow morning. We can find a lot more than most people think. Most people, namely arsonists, think they can get away with it as long as the fire's big enough and hot enough. Not so. There's always evidence to be found."

"Well," the sheriff said, "I sure appreciate you coming by."

The man stood. "Gotta go," he said. "I've got to get on back to Dallas. We'll have a crew out there tomorrow, and believe me, my boys will sift through the whole dang thing. If there's a scrap of evidence there, we'll find it. Pleased to meet you, Judge."

Jackson nodded and the man left.

Dooley woke up and scooted his chair up to the desk.

The sheriff got up and refilled his coffee mug. He poured one for Jackson and brought it to him.

"Reckon that blows away Mr. Tad Padgett's gonna-get-famous case," the sheriff commented.

"Does Tad know?" Jackson asked.

"Yeah. Reedy reported to him before he came here."

The men sipped their coffee in silence for a while, each thinking his own thoughts. Jackson glanced over at Dooley, who was sitting with his usual bovine expression, chewing on a purple toothpick. Unmistakably, it came from Dickie's Deli.

"Been patronizing the deli?" Jackson asked.

"Who me? Naw. I'm a Dairy Star man, myself."

"Where'd you get that toothpick then?"

"Had it," Dooley said. "Picked it up the night old Tom Delgado got smoked."

The sheriff looked at him. "How come it looks so new? You mostly chew them things down to a nub."

Dooley sighed as if he were in the company of morons. "On account of, I ain't wore this shirt since March. I keep me a spare in all my shirt pockets." He took the toothpick out of his mouth and looked at it. He popped it back in. "Seems like this here shirt got shoved 'way back in my closet, doncha know. I just forgot I had the damn thing."

Dooley was a single man, and was casual about the clothes he wore. Sometimes Norma Jean made him bring his shirts in to be washed and ironed by her, because she got tired of seeing him coming around in rough-dried clothing.

"You picked that up at Tom's office?" Jackson said.

"Yes, sir. That's what I just told you."

"Exactly where in the office?"

Dooley scratched his head. "Lemme see now. Oh, yeah. It was right in front of old Tom's desk. I seen it there on the carpet and just picked it up." He looked at the sheriff, who was glaring at him. "Nothin' wrong with that. It was just an old toothpick."

"It was evidence, you birdbrain."

The sheriff and Jackson looked at each other. If that toothpick was in Tom's office, it could mean only one thing. Dickie had lied when he said he hadn't been past the door.

The sheriff took a brown envelope from his desk drawer and handed it to Dooley. "Let's have it."

Dooley spit the toothpick into the envelope and handed it back to the sheriff.

"Dickie said he never made it into that office," Sheriff Gibbs said slowly. "He said he stayed in the outer office. Matter of fact, Brenda Barns said the same thing."

"Still," Jackson said, "somebody else

might have dropped it there. Tell you what. I'll call Fayrene Moses. She told me she was cleaning up in there only a short time before Tom was killed. Maybe she remembers something."

He picked up the phone and dialed a number. He spoke briefly with Fayrene.

When he hung up, he looked at the other two men. "Fayrene is sure she was the last one in that office until the murderer came. And she swears there was no toothpick on the floor."

"A toothpick is mighty slim evidence," the sheriff said.

Jackson took the folded printout from his pocket and passed it to the sheriff.

The sheriff's face froze. "Come on," he said. "Let's get him. You comin', Judge?"

Jackson stood up. "No, but I'd like to sit in when he gives his statement."

Jackson went home while Sheriff Gibbs and Dooley went off to arrest Dickie Deaver.

Chapter Eighteen

Dickie Deaver's Statement

I was born to a wealthy family in San Francisco. My father, who had come from poor folks, was a self-made man. He became a lawyer and was cofounder of a prestigious law firm. They practiced corporate law and were more than successful at it. It was the typical rich-kid existence, prep schools, country club living, travel abroad. Then after high school, my brother and I were sent east to college, Harvard for him, Princeton for me. It was our dad's plan that we both finish law school and then join the law firm. He wanted a dynasty, and we were it.

My brother, Sam, took to the law like he was born to it, which he was. I was a different story. My grades were average; my heart wasn't in it. Dad never even noticed. He was so focused on his dream that he couldn't see how miserable I was. Well, like a lot of kids, I turned to alcohol, and later experimented with drugs. I was a party animal. Finally, Mom convinced Dad that I was having problems, so he called me in for one of his "talks." That meant he did the talking and you did the listening. He told me to either get my act together or get out of Dodge. Oddly, that talk took with me. No, I was never going to be the big corporate lawyer, but I did quit the drugs. I also quit school and got myself a job at one of the exclusive Italian restaurants in town — as a cook's helper. In my case, that meant kitchen slave and dishwasher. I didn't mind. The minute I walked into the commercial kitchen, I knew I had found my bliss. I wanted to own a place like that and to be a chef.

I saved my money, got student loans, and enrolled in culinary school. There, I shone. I made the best grades in my class and was named the finest pastry chef the school had ever taught.

Foolishly, I took my honors home to my parents, hoping for a little recognition from them. My father ordered me out of the house and announced that I would be cut out of his will. I never saw them again, but somehow that didn't hurt me much. I was doing what I loved.

As time passed, I was able to get a bank loan and I opened a little bistro in a trendy district of town. Customers came in droves. I married the sweetest girl in the world, and she was happy to work side by side with me in the business. I thought I was making it. And I guess I would have been, if I had been a businessman. The problem was I was a chef. I hired financial advisers. They bilked me for everything I had. I fired them and kept on trying to go it alone. It was about that time that Tom Delgado came into my life.

He used to come into my place regularly, usually with a table full of friends and business associates. Tom wore expensive clothes and Italian shoes. He was obviously a success at something — what, I didn't know. I wondered sometimes if he was involved with the mob.

One night, when I was closing, Tom came in alone. He asked me to pour him a drink and stay open while he drank it. For such a good customer, I was glad to comply. We sat and talked for a long time that night. I confided in him how much trouble I was in, and he seemed genuinely sympathetic, offering suggestions for how I could get solvent again. I poured him another drink and one for myself.

After a while, Tom made me an offer.

"I'm starting a new venture," he said. "It can't fail."

"What kind of venture?" I wanted to know.

And he explained it to me. It would be a brand-new long-distance service. This was right after deregulation, and new companies were cropping up all over the place. But this one would be different. There was a brand-new, innovative marketing plan. I'll admit, I was intrigued.

"Tell me more," I said, pouring us both another drink.

"What you do is, you get your customers involved," he said. "You sell to them, they sell to others, and they get to keep part of the money, but part of it comes back to you. Then those others sell, and you get a portion of their sales. It can go on indefinitely, and the money just keeps pouring into the company. We can't lose. Nobody's ever done this with telecommunications before. Oh, sure, they've sold household products and women's makeup that way, but that's small potatoes. With us there'll be no products to schlep around; all we do is hook people up. And on top of that, we get the monthly fees for the service. And here's my offer to you. I'll make you president of the corporation. I'll be in the background acting as chief financial officer."

My head was spinning. I knew nothing about business, but Tom was so fired up about it, I got excited, too. I pictured myself being successful in this venture and shoving it in my father's face.

Finally, I came back to reality. "But all I ever wanted to do was run a nice restaurant," I said.

"That's the beauty of it," he said. "You sell this place, invest the money in our project, and within a year, you'll be able to cash out and buy you a really nice place. A *four-star* restaurant. Think about that!"

I did, and it sounded like the chance of a lifetime. I joined him.

My wife was dubious, but she could see that I wasn't going to change my mind. We sold the restaurant for a nice profit and gave the money to Tom.

Well, long story short, the money started rolling in just as Tom had promised. We bought a nice house, a boat, and a brand-new BMW. I was living high. Then the hammer fell.

It was a pyramid scheme, pure and simple. The feds were on to us in less than a year. Interstate commerce, you know. The trial was all over the papers. Lots of people had been hurt. Now I knew why Tom Delgado had been so generous as to let me be president. I was the one to fall first. They gave me ten years. Tom copped a plea and got off with probation and a fine.

My wife left me while I was in prison. Sent me a "Dear John."

Well, I learned a lot in there, but I kept my nose clean and was let out in four for good behavior. I stood on the sidewalk in front of that prison and made a decision. I was going back to doing what I loved. I had managed to stash away a few thousand that nobody knew about. I took that money and left California for good.

I didn't know exactly what had happened to Tom. I knew he had gone out of state and married himself a rich wife. I'd heard that he had started up another business, but I didn't know and didn't care what it was. All I wanted was a new start in a new place, where nobody knew anything about me.

I used part of my money to get a little used car and took off across the country. I knew what I was doing. I was scouting for likely places to settle, out-of-the-way places, places like Post Oak. The first time I drove down Main Street, I felt at home. I saw a FOR RENT sign on the building I'm in now, and immediately called the number. I was amazed at how cheaply you could rent a storefront out here in the boonies. I cleaned it up, bought some secondhand equipment, and, you know the rest. Dickie's Deli was born.

It wasn't until I'd been here for six or seven months that I happened to see one of Tom's signs around town. I was furious. What twist of fate had sent me to the very town where that bastard had set up shop? But what could I do? I had already invested all I had in this business. I had to stay, and if he lived here, too, so be it. Naturally, we ran into each other. Tom told me how sorry he was the way everything worked out, and he hoped we could put the past behind us. That's the way we left it. He would throw business my way whenever he felt like it. Guilt, I guess.

I wasn't letting my anger eat away at me. My little deli was growing every day, and I was busy putting my heart and soul into it. Then one day, Tom dropped by to see me — and wrote out his own death warrant.

"Brother," he said.

Brother? I thought. *What was that all about? He'd never called me that before.*

"Brother, I want to witness to you. I found salvation when I accepted Jesus Christ as my personal savior."

"Congratulations." I didn't know what to say.

"And my sins are forgiven," he went on. "All of them." He looked hard at me, and I knew what he meant.

I didn't have an answer for that, but Tom didn't care. He had more to say.

"I want you to accept the Lord into your heart, old friend."

I wanted to punch him in the face. Old friend, my ass! Who did he think he was talking to? But it was a slow time, so I let him rattle on. I was only half listening until I heard him say. "Now all I have to do is make my public confession before the whole congregation of the Reverend Mary Dobbs McDermott's cathedral in Dallas, then I can be baptized in the Spirit."

"What?"

"I'm telling it all," he said. "I'll be pure as the driven snow."

And I'll be up shit creek, I thought. "Naming names?" I stammered.

"Names and all," he said, throwing his arms wide. "Names and all. The Reverend Sister says you have to come clean before the Lord and His people."

Well, anyone could see that I couldn't let that happen. Hadn't I been through enough? I couldn't let Tom Delgado go before that congregation, so I shot him. I got to his office early that day. Tom was there, and he let me in. All I had to do was follow him back into his office and shoot him. Then I went back outside, locked the door behind me, and waited. Brenda Barns drove up, and I told her I couldn't get in. I thought it was the perfect alibi, and it would have been if it hadn't been for those confounded toothpicks.

I felt bad about it, of course. I'd never killed a person in my life. But it had to be done. And I thought I'd covered my tracks pretty well. Turned out, I was wrong. Anyway, after a while, I got to thinking about that preacher lady. What if Tom had already done his confessing to her? What if she knew? It was a shame, but she had to go, too. I waited for her outside of town; when I got a chance, I shot her.

After that I felt safe again — for a little while.

Dossie Delgado had come home from the jail and began calling me to order food now and then. I felt so sorry for the woman — and guilty, too, of course. I'd been the one to put her where she was. Sometimes, when I brought the food, she would want to talk. She was really steamed about how things had turned out. And drinking helped to drive away the anger. I never drank with her, but I'd sit for hours listening to her talk.

One night, she told me that Tom had told her all about the long-distance business and my involvement in it. I poured her another drink. When she was too drunk to navigate, I helped her up to her bed and waited until she had passed out. I went downstairs and found some charcoal lighter fluid. I sprayed it all over the drapes and set them afire. Then, for good measure, I sprayed the bed and lit it, too.

Chapter Nineteen

Jackson put down the statement and looked across his desk at the sheriff and Tad Padgett. Dooley sat a little to the side, his hat over his eyes.

"Don't that just frost your butt?" the sheriff said. "Him such a runty little feller, too."

"You just never know," said Tad, looking sad. "I thought I had me a big case to try. Now, this."

"Son, you oughta be proud. We just cleaned up three murders in one day."

"I know, Sheriff. But I really wanted to try this one."

"But she wasn't guilty," the sheriff argued. "You might have lost — or even worse, you might have won."

Tad looked sheepish. "Hadn't thought of that," he mumbled.

"So, how did he respond when you showed up at his door?" Jackson asked.

The sheriff hitched up his pants and shifted in his chair. "He was getting ready to clear out," he said. "When we got there, we saw a CLOSED sign on the front door, so we drove around back to where he had a door to his living quarters. Opens from the alley, doncha know."

"He's got it fixed up real nice," Dooley piped in. "Green painted door and little potted trees on either side of it."

"Go back to sleep," the sheriff said. "Well, sir, we pounded on the door right loud, and he opened it straightaway. I asked if we could come in, and he let us. He was packing in there. Getting ready to flee, is what I was thinking. We showed him the warrant and read him his rights, but I no mor'n got the words out of my mouth than he commenced to talking. We brought him in and took his statement, and still he wanted to talk. For all I know he's still talking down in his jail cell. That little peckerwood had a lot to get off his chest. I swear to God, I think he was relieved to see us comin'."

"Well, that's it for me," Tad said. "I've got a hot date tonight. You boys wish me luck. This gal's a real fox."

"I've got to go, too; the wife's got supper ready. Come on, Dooley." The sheriff stood up.

"Wait," Jackson said. "What about the gun?"

"We got that," the sheriff said. "He just handed it over. Lab's got it now. Hell, I hope they get it right this time."

Jackson sat at his desk and watched as the three men left. He got up and went out, locking the door behind him.

As he pulled in to his driveway, he saw that Lutie's car was not in its usual spot. Choir practice, he thought. That meant a cold supper for him and Patty. He went into the kitchen and found a note on the table. "Cold cuts in the fridge. Patty's gone to Lamaze classes with Ashley and her mama."

He walked over to the telephone and found a message from Roxanne. "Come out for supper." Her voice sounded strange, as warm as usual, but a little tense. Jackson wondered what was up. He dialed her number, and when the answering machine picked up, said that he would be out at seven.

Upstairs in his room, he showered and dressed in casual clothes. The clock on the dresser said only six, so he went downstairs, poured himself a Scotch, and waited until it was time to go.

His mind went back to Dickie Deaver. The poor son of a bitch. He wondered how much his time in prison had to do with his willingness to kill and kill again to reach his own ends. Was he that kind of a guy when he started out? Were you born with the capacity to murder — or was it something you picked up along the way? As Jackson saw it, Dovie was the only innocent victim. The other two, Tom and Mary Dobbs Mc-Dermott, were cut from the same cloth. Both were hustlers in their own way. They were a ruthless pair who would let nothing, even destroying innocent lives, get in their way. And their goals were not all that different either, the lust for money and power. Dovie alone had wanted nothing more than to live out her life quietly with the man she loved.

Jackson looked at the clock on the wall. Time to go.

When he arrived at the Kruger ranch, Roxanne was waiting on the front porch for him, as usual. Without saying anything, she kissed him softly and took him by the hand, leading him into the front hallway. What he saw made his heart sink.

"What's all this?" he asked, knowing before he asked what the crated paintings and luggage piled neatly next to the front door meant.

"It's time," she said.

"No." The word stuck in his throat.

"Jackson, come into the parlor and let me pour you a glass of wine. You're white as a sheet."

He followed her numbly into the room and took the glass she offered him.

"Sit here," she said, patting the sofa cushion next to her. "Jackson, you knew I would be leaving someday." She sipped her wine. "I've put the house on the market. I'll be leaving early tomorrow. I couldn't leave without having one more evening with you."

"But why now? I thought you were enjoying yourself here."

"Enjoying myself? Of course I am. I'm having the time of my life. But I've told you how important my work is to me. Well, it's finished. Fall will be here soon, and I need to get back to my studio and prepare these pieces for showing. It's a big job."

Jackson was getting angry. "And you're just selling your father's ranch. The place he built with his own hands."

She threw up her hands. "What am I going to do with it? My life is someplace else."

"Come back here. Stay summers . . . something."

"No. I know myself. I'd never do that. Cape Cod, Maine, Europe, those are the places I spend my free time. It's better for someone else to have the ranch, someone who'll love it the way Daddy did."

"Then I'm never going to see you again."

"Oh, Jackson. Don't say never. Nobody knows what the future holds. Anything can happen." She stood up. "Come on, Cookie's laid out supper in the kitchen."

They ate fried quail and a delicious vegetable terrine at the kitchen table. They shared another bottle of wine, made love on her bed, and then said a long good-bye at the front door.

EPILOGUE

Three Months Later

Jackson pulled his car into the carport and stopped. As soon as he got out he caught the scent of chicken frying in the kitchen. He hoped Lutie would make her famous smashed potatoes and gravy to go with it.

Patty met him at the door.

"Daddy, guess what! I'm going to be a godmother!"

"Well." He hugged her. "How about that? What does a godmother do, anyway?"

"Brother Steve says you have to pray for the kid all the time and give them gifts on their birthday. I can do that, no problem."

"I didn't know Baptists had godparents."

"They don't. Brother Steve has decided he wants to be an Episcopal deacon. He's studying for that now."

"Well, congratulations, then." He put his briefcase down on the hall bench and went into the kitchen, where he found Lutie busy

266

at the stove. Patty followed him.

"Daddy, can I go over to Ashley's after supper?"

"It's a school night."

"I know, but we're going to study. I need to help her with her algebra. You know how good I am at that. Vanessa's been doing a good job homeschooling her, but she doesn't know anything about algebra, and Brother Steve says his is rustier than an old horseshoe nail. Will you drive me over there? Brother Steve will bring me home early."

"Okay, then."

When they got to the old Rice mansion, they found Steve and Vanessa putting a mountain of supper dishes into their big, commercial-size dishwasher.

"Sit down, Jackson," Steve said. "We'll be through here in a minute. We'll make some coffee and have a good visit."

"So, you're switching sides, I hear," Jackson said.

"Well, I wouldn't exactly say that. Baptists and Episcopalians are both on God's side," Steve said with a laugh. "I just got interested in the denomination and its history. Got to talking to Father John over at St. Stephen's and decided to make the jump."

Vanessa groaned. "They have services at nine, and Steve expects me to have all the kids dressed and ready at that time."

"Do not," Steve said, winking at Jackson.

"Do, too," she said, punching him affectionately.

When he got back home, Jackson went into his den, poured himself a Scotch, and, sinking into his chair, lit a Don Diego. He thought about the Largents. They worked like slaves from sunup to sundown, and yet always seemed to be in good spirits. They were a team in every way and still as much in love as the day they met. How did they do it? And why couldn't he have that?

He thought about Gretchen, Patty's mother. They had been so much in love when they married just out of college. She was a wonderful wife and mother, always sunny and cheerful. And then cancer had taken her, and he had watched as she faded away. She had died so long ago, and they had both been so young, that he had no idea how they would have finished out their lives together. Now she was just a distant memory.

He thought about Mandy. He missed her still. She had fit him like a kid glove. They had laughed at the same things, agreed on most things, and both enjoyed quiet times together when talking was optional. Yet, what they had must not have been enough for her. Was it him? Was he boring? Did women need more excitement than he had to give? Well, he was what he was, and that was not going to change.

He thought about Roxanne and the magical times they had had last summer. He had gotten up happy and gone to sleep happy at night. Each day was a new adventure with her. She was intelligent and strong and immensely talented. She was kind; she was beautiful. She was quicksilver. Could he have held on to her, even if she had been willing to try? Well, he'd never know.

He finished his Scotch and poured another, feeling extremely sorry for himself.

And then the telephone rang.

ABOUT THE AUTHOR

Nancy Bell is the author of the celebrated Biggie Weatherford mystery series. This is her third cozy in the Judge Jackson Crain series; previous titles included *Restored to Death* and *Death Splits a Hair.* She lives in Pittsburg, Texas.

The employees of Thorndike Press hope you have enjoyed this Large Print book. All our Thorndike and Wheeler Large Print titles are designed for easy reading, and all our books are made to last. Other Thorndike Press Large Print books are available at your library, through selected bookstores, or directly from us.

For information about titles, please call:
    (800) 223-1244

or visit our Web site at:
    http://gale.cengage.com/thorndike

To share your comments, please write:
    Publisher
    Thorndike Press
    295 Kennedy Memorial Drive
    Waterville, ME 04901